the drawback of single dads

PIPER RAYNE

Cover Design: By Hang Le

Cover Photo: Lindee Robinson Photography

1st Line Editor: Joy Editing

2nd Line Editor: My Brother's Editor

Proofreader: My Brother's Editor

He's the father of my child and my best friend.

When Hudson and I met, somehow things just clicked between us. We had the same sense of humor and the same carefree attitude about our lives and goals. Neither of us wanted to lay down roots, we wanted to explore the world.

Then one night, too much alcohol and uncontrolled hormones led to the line blurring, and we fell into bed together only to discover a month later that we were more careless than we thought.

Like the upstanding guy he is, Hudson followed me back to my hometown of Lake Starlight, Alaska, where you can't throw a penny and not hit one of my family members. We gave them the news that yes, we were having a baby but there would be no wedding. We loved each other but we weren't in love.

Fast forward three years and we live side by side to make co-parenting our daughter easy. I'm a writer, and he's a ski instructor. We've worked out all the rough edges. Life is good.

Until out of nowhere, things start to change. He has a girlfriend, we're arguing more than ever, and it feels as if someone has come along and popped our perfect bubble.

I'm not sure we're ever going to fit back inside it now because things are developing. Things like feelings.

The Drawback of *Single Dads*

one

PALMER

I press the delete key on my computer over and over, erasing the only two sentences I've managed to squeeze out in the last hour. My forehead falls to the keyboard.

This is it. My short writing career is over.

If I can't write two decent sentences, how will I ever have a manuscript to turn in to my editor in two months? I won't be able to pay my bills. I'll lose the house. I won't be able to clothe or feed Adley.

A whirl of cold air gushes through the back door, alerting me that someone's here. Winter has officially arrived in my small town of Lake Starlight, Alaska.

I grab my cochlear implants and put them on.

My parents had tried to get me the implants when I was younger, but I wasn't a candidate, but as technology advanced over the decades, that changed.

I don't bother standing because I know who's coming in, and the two of them have been used to seeing me in this exact position for the past several months.

Hudson sits on the chair next to me and stares at me

with those judgmental eyes. Does my best friend really think writing a novel is so simple? Maybe he should try it sometime. The man makes his living gallivanting around ski slopes. I glance around, searching for our brown-haired little girl.

He says, "She's with Theresa. They'll be over in five."

I nod, standing and lifting my coffee mug.

He follows me into the kitchen and grabs the pot before I can. "How many have you already had?"

I roll my eyes and swipe at the pot, but he holds it up high. I sigh, but his smirk says he's not going to give in until I answer.

Setting my mug down, I lift my hands and sign, *Three. Sue me, it's crunch time.*

He chuckles, pouring my cup of coffee, his jokester face on the entire time. "One day, you'll need an IV to get enough." Grabbing his own cup from the cabinet above the sink, he pours himself a cup, goes to the fridge, and grabs some milk to put in. Again, he shakes his head at the lonely items in my fridge. "And I trust you to take care of our daughter? Good thing I'm only next door."

I roll my eyes again and give him a vulgar gesture before heading to the kitchen table. After taking a sip, I put my cup on the table and lift my hands. Although I have cochlear implants, I still sign a lot. Force of habit, I guess. Plus, Hudson and I have always signed in front of Adley, even if we're talking to help her learn, along with the weekly class she takes.

Let me guess, you made her a three-course breakfast with freshly squeezed orange juice? I lift my eyebrows because when she stays at his place, Adley usually has a Pop-Tart in hand as she goes out the door, hair barely brushed.

His lips tip up, and he looks out the window toward his

house before he takes a seat across from me. "Theresa brought breakfast over this morning."

She didn't spend the night, right?

"No. I'm abiding by the rules."

I'm just saying it seems like it's getting serious.

"Um...not sure about that."

I kick him under the table. *I bet you the time is coming.*

"Time for what?"

She's going to want more.

I love Hudson. He's my best friend. The lines blurred one drunken night, and that's how we were blessed with Adley, our three-year-old daughter. Just as I knew he would, he stepped up, leaving his nomad life to settle down in my hometown of Lake Starlight. He even bought the house next to mine so we could raise her together.

Hudson isn't the kind of guy who wants to settle down, so his commitment to his daughter is usually what pulls on the heartstrings of his conquests first. Unless it's his thick, dirty-blond hair that's only ever styled by his fingers and the scruff along his jaw that grabs their attention first. My best friend isn't hard on the eyes.

"She knows where we stand."

I sip my coffee and stare at him over the rim of the mug.

"You have no idea what you're talking about." I can tell by the tone of his voice that he knows he's grown closer to Theresa than any other woman he's taken to his bed.

Theresa has a six-year-old daughter, and she's a teacher, so she's one of those women born knowing how to interact with children the minute she meets them. I don't know how far she's wormed her way into my daughter's heart, but since Hudson has kept her around this long, I have to wonder if she's wormed her way into his. I rub my chest.

"What's the matter?" Hudson's eyes follow the movement of my hand.

Heartburn.

He laughs. "Coffee and a crap diet will do that."

More cold air wafts into the house, and the vibration on the floor of little feet running warms my heart. Even though she's only been next door for the past two days, I've missed her. I put my coffee down and turn in my chair, ready for her to run into my arms, but Adley stops right before she reaches me.

"Mommy, look what Theresa gave me!" She holds out a lipstick, and that's when I notice the red all over her lips.

"Oh, lipstick," I say aloud.

A knock sounds on my back door.

Why doesn't she just come in? I sign to Hudson.

"I don't know." He stands and reaches to ruffle Adley's hair, but she ducks so he misses.

I can see why. It's beautiful, woven in two braids that come together in the back. I could never pull it off. I guarantee Adley's preschool teachers will know who got Adley ready this morning just based on her hairstyle alone.

I sign to Adley. *Come here.*

I open my arms, and she runs into them, squeezing me hard. I kiss her cheek, and she does the same to me before drawing back and laughing at the red lips she's left there.

There are muffled voices as Hudson opens the door for Theresa. I can't hear what they're saying, but by the time they reach us at the kitchen table, Theresa looks flustered with Hudson. The two of them couldn't be more opposite. Hudson is laid back, and Theresa just isn't. There's nothing wrong with that, but it surprised me the first time I saw them together. Hudson doesn't mind dirty dishes and folded laundry on the couch, and Theresa is always very put together. I imagine her house looks like a home decorating catalog.

"Look!" Adley points at the red lips on my cheek.

"Oh, I'm sorry. She was watching me freshen up after breakfast and asked if she could have some." Theresa clutches Hudson's arm as if she's afraid he might leave her alone with me.

I lift my hands. *It's okay. Thanks for making her breakfast.*

She looks at Hudson, and he translates for me. These are times I should speak, but I've never been comfortable hearing my own voice.

Theresa shoots me one of her plastic smiles. "You're welcome."

I smile back and nod. That's about the extent of my conversations with Theresa, though I don't blame her. She shouldn't be expected to learn sign language just because the baby mama of the guy she's dating is deaf.

"Mommy!" Adley pulls on my shirt. "Theresa said she could take me to school today."

I glance at my laptop sitting on the table. I never work here, but this morning, I thought maybe being in a different spot than my couch would make the words fly out of me. There's a plate with half a tuna sandwich on it with five Cosmic Brownie wrappers on top. Yeah, I'll have to break it to Adley that I dug into her Little Debbie stash. Not the first time. Won't be the last.

I catch Theresa looking back at me after following my line of vision to my three in the morning snack. I lift my hands, and Theresa automatically looks at Hudson. *I've got it, but please tell her thanks.*

Hudson gives no expression as he tells Theresa, and her eyes focus on me. "I didn't mean to upset anyone."

You didn't.

After Hudson tells her what I signed, he puts his hand on the small of her back. "Let's go."

Theresa seems reluctant at first but eventually walks out of my house without saying anything.

Hudson crouches down, and Adley wraps her arms around his neck. "Have a good day at school and please keep your hands to yourself. I can't keep giving Mr. Grier free ski lessons to keep you there."

Adley smiles one of her wicked ones. The one that says she's not making any promises. She likes this boy named Holden and tries to kiss him every day at recess. "He likes me too."

Adley runs into her room to grab her coat and backpack. Hudson nods, pushing his fingers through his hair.

*Hey, she gets it from you. The last man in my bed was…*I let it hang there because it's embarrassing how long ago that was.

"You want me to remind you how you were back in the day before I knocked you up?"

You know how I love the phrase knocked up.

"I'm just saying you were just as horny as me."

But now you're settling down. I can hear all the ski bunnies on the mountain crying from here.

"Theresa knows the score. She's not going to ask me to change."

I raise my eyebrows. *Okay then.*

"I have a new client today, so I gotta get to the slopes. I'll see you later, and maybe if you got a little, that romance book of yours would write itself."

As if sex solves everything.

"At least go somewhere and get out of your head."

I wave goodbye, and he huffs, shutting the door behind him. I pour myself a to-go cup of coffee and watch Hudson saying goodbye to Theresa. He embraces her, and they kiss, but it doesn't last long before they separate, and he waves, going inside his house.

She walks carefully so as not to slip on the icy concrete of his driveway, then climbs into her compact SUV and reverses down the driveway. She's almost too perfect. She must save her toenail clippings or something gross that no one would ever suspect. No one can be as perfect as she is.

After she's gone, I clean off my cheek and Adley's lips, then I get her into my Jeep and drive to her preschool. She sings to the music, pointing at things out of the window, while my mind continues to try to work out this story. I have no choice but to call my editor and face her wrath.

The best thing about Adley's preschool is you drop off without having to leave the car line. So she unbuckles when we reach the point, climbs between the seats to kiss me on the cheek as always, and exits out of the back door after the helper opens it. I wave and smile, driving off.

The worst thing about Adley's preschool is that I only have about two and a half hours to get to whatever I need to do before she's done. Heading into town, I park my car along Main Street and go into Lard Have Mercy, needing a coffee and a muffin to tide me over. But I didn't think this through, because as soon as I'm through the door, a bunch of people in the back call my name.

Shit.

It's a group of my cousins. Since there are so many of us, we've naturally split into smaller groups, and the ones here are what have always been referred to as the Bailey Triplets. Although all three were born to a different set of my aunts and uncles, they were all born within the same twenty-four hours, hence the nickname.

I walk over, concerned they'll keep me here the entire time Adley's in school.

Lance slides over in the booth to make room for me.

"What's up, Palmer?" Easton stands to hug me. "I'll be right back." He heads into the restroom.

"How's it going?" Brinley asks, tucking her long blonde hair behind her ear.

It's not that busy in here this morning, so I can hear them fine with my implants. Maggie hands me my muffin and sets a to-go coffee on the table, knowing my usual.

"I'm behind on the deadline. Can't get into the story," I say.

Brinley and Lance share a look.

"What?" I look between them.

"We have just the solution," Lance says, laying his tie back in place now that he's finished eating.

"What?" None of them are writers, so I can't imagine what they have in mind.

"You have time to go on a short drive?" Brinley asks.

This is just the thing I was dreading. But since I'll do about anything in an attempt to get this book done, of course I say, "Sure."

HUDSON

I walk into the ski lodge and find Matt Peterson waiting for me in a comfy brown leather chair in front of the roaring fire. He's already grabbed the attention of a woman who isn't dressed in snow gear, which could mean she doesn't even know she's talking to a gold medal snowboarder.

Matt is nearing the end of his career, but demanding one more go at a medal. So he sought me out to help him come up with some new moves to impress the judges. It feels a little odd, since for the past four years I've only been a ski instructor, but before Palmer got knocked up and we had Adley, I'd been a big deal, at least in the extreme snow sports arena.

Matt sees me and nods, quickly dismissing the woman. What does he care? He'll have another whenever he wants. The man has the reputation of a playboy.

"Hey, man." We shake hands.

I nod toward the woman who's across the room now. "And who's that?"

He shakes his head, his dark hair tumbling over his eyes

for a second. "Just some slope bunny pretending she doesn't know who I am."

"Strike one," I say, knowing his MO. "How did you know?"

"She asked me how I liked boarding in Beijing." He laughs. "She didn't even realize how much she fucked up."

Both of us look in her direction to find her gaze still on Matt.

"And I didn't tell her. Come on, I'm anxious to get out there." He walks by me to the doors, and I wave to the people I know.

I fall in line with him, both of us grabbing our boards on the way out. "Still not settling down?"

"Still playing daddy?" He raises an eyebrow.

"I am a dad, so there is no playing."

He laughs. "Not many would give up what you did."

"She's worth it all and then some." I grab my phone out of my pocket and pull up Adley's picture.

He looks at it, then at me. "Adorable."

But as with most reactions from Matt, I can't figure out if he's being sarcastic or not. I don't think he's the type to ever settle down. He's more the perpetual playboy who will die doing some crazy stunt at seventy-nine or something.

"I know. She's the best."

His gaze bounces to my left hand. "At least you're still single."

"I am, but I'm seeing someone."

He holds his board while we wait for the lift. "I shouldn't be surprised, I guess."

A minute later, we're sitting in the warm gondola, moving up the mountain. "Why wouldn't you be surprised?"

He chuckles as if there's an inside joke only he knows. "I

took an Uber into downtown Lake Starlight last night, and there doesn't seem to be anything crazy to do except get drunk and get a stupid tattoo. The stares I got when I walked into that bar, Lucky's." He shakes his head.

"I thought you'd be used to stares by now."

"Not stares like I walked into a private party during a speech. Finally, it got a little better when the owner, Van, offered me an empty stool and a drink on the house."

I laugh. "Van is my baby mama's cousin's husband."

"He's what?" He chuckles. "I forgot you moved here because of her and her big-ass family."

The gondola is almost to the top, so we prepare to get out. "I like my life." I step out first, with Matt right behind me.

"But do you love it?" His eyebrows rise as he secures his helmet and pulls down his goggles.

"I love the people, yes," I answer as honestly as I can.

I do love Lake Starlight, and at first it was an adjustment, getting used to running into people, most of whom were Palmer's relatives, everywhere I went. But Adley changed my life, and I can't imagine not living wherever Palmer is. I get that Matt doesn't see much value in that, but maybe when he's done setting records and claiming gold medals, he'll feel differently.

"I love my mom, but I wanted the hell out of my hometown."

Not wanting to continue this conversation, I bring it back to the reason we're here. "Let's get you in line for the halfpipe."

We wait since we can't reserve it especially for Matt, even though he's an icon in the sport. Anyway, it will be good to go over his tricks before he does his run again.

"I've set up a friend to videotape, so I want you to do whatever you want, then I'll give you my thoughts."

"Perfect." He walks over to some kids probably twenty years his junior, and most of them know who he is, giving him high fives and fist bumps.

I sit back and wait, but I don't have to wait too long because each kid in line allows Matt to go in front. Matt, being Matt, takes the opportunity they're giving him.

His first run is good but not great. Right off, it's clear he isn't getting the height he needs to do the big tricks this sport demands nowadays. Every year the tricks get scarier, athletes doing the unthinkable when one false move could kill them.

I didn't tell Matt, but seeing Adley grow up is dream number one for me now. I just can't put my life at risk the way he does, knowing it would be my fault if I left her without a dad because I'm an adrenaline junkie.

When he's back up the mountain, he walks over to me, shaking his head. "Fuck, you don't have to tell me. I barely got enough air on the first trick." His goggles rest on his helmet, and he looks at me for advice.

Sometimes I wonder why he sought me out after all these years when half of my day is spent teaching families and kids who have never skied how to use the pizza method to control their speed. We chat about the changes he can make and go through a few more runs, his improvement showing by the third time.

After his last run, I snowboard to the bottom to meet him, and someone calls my name. I turn to find Palmer's cousin Harper.

The entire Bailey clan can ski or snowboard like champs, which I guess happens when you grow up in Alaska. Ironically, Palmer can't. She always refused to learn for some reason, but at least she trusts me on the slopes with Adley.

"Hey, Harper," I say when she comes over with some of her friends. All their attention is on Matt instead of me.

"Do you know Matt Peterson?" I ask them.

As a group, they say yes and nod, a few of them giggling. Harper shakes her head at them. She's been around me when I've had some other professional athletes come to me for training and tips.

"Hey, girls," Matt says.

"Hi," they say in unison with the typical flirty girl voices I'm sure Matt expects.

I introduce Matt to Harper, and she says each of her friend's names, each one unable to take their eyes off Matt.

When was the last time I was looked at like they wanted to tie me up naked and explore my entire body twice?

My phone rings in my pocket, so I grab it to see it's the school.

"Excuse me," I say and walk a few steps away while swiping my phone. "Hello?"

"Hi, this is Marcie again."

"What did she do?" I ask, knowing Adley couldn't keep her hands to herself.

"Adley chased another student around the playground, asking him to kiss her."

I blow out a breath.

"Mr. Grier would like for you and Miss Bailey to come in again and have another conversation."

"Do I need to pick her up right now?" I can't cancel my lessons for the day again. This is Palmer's job today, her day with Adley. "Did you try to call Palmer?"

"We did, but we didn't get an answer. No need to get Adley, though. Mr. Grier assured me we'd figure this out during the conference. Get in touch with Miss Ferguson and let me know a good time for the two of you to come in." There's a trace of humor in Marcie's voice, suggesting she finds this whole thing funny. My three-year-old chasing boys around asking them to kiss her? Not funny at all.

"Thanks, Marcie, I'll be in touch."

I hang up and call Palmer immediately. It rings and rings and goes to her voicemail. She must have her phone on Do Not Disturb. I pocket my phone, shaking my head, and go back over to the group.

"Trouble in Domestic Ville?" Matt asks with a shit-eating grin.

Harper's eyes pinch together, and she looks at me. *Harper, did you really think Matt Peterson was going to fall madly in love with you and marry you after meeting him at the base of the mountain?*

"No. But I have another lesson I have to get to. You want to come by for dinner tonight?"

"Depends, do I get to meet the little lady?"

"Which one?" Harper asks, causing me to turn in her direction.

"Oh, maybe things do get a little crazy in Domestic Ville?" Matt eyes me.

"Theresa. Palmer is just Adley's mom. We're not involved like that."

Harper rolls her eyes and smiles. "Yeah okay, you keep telling yourself that. Come on, ladies, let's go check out the halfpipe. Bye, Matt. Bye, Hudson." She waves her gloved hand and all of them head in the direction we just came from.

"Ignore her. She doesn't know what she's talking about."

"Sure, she doesn't. Text me the address and time and

what to bring. I've been dying for a home-cooked meal." He slaps me on the shoulder. "In the meantime, I'm going to work up an appetite." His eyes follow a woman walking on her own before he turns and waves, falling in line with her.

I shake my head and walk toward the bunny hill where I'll be teaching little kids for the rest of the day. On the way, I pull out my cell phone and message Theresa with the hopes that she can come over and cook a meal Matt will love. I have a few things in my repertoire, but Theresa is a master in the kitchen. Plus, it's our two nights where both our girls are with their other parent.

> My new client is coming over for dinner tonight. I'm willing to wager a deal if you're willing to cook.

The three dots appear.

> Tell me the new client isn't spending the night too.

> Does that mean you want to be paid back in the bedroom?

> Maybe.

> How about I do the dishes and then I do you?

> Sounds good. I'll stop at the store on my way over.

> Thanks. ;)

When we first started dating, Theresa was more casual and carefree. Sure, she's always been a type A personality, but it wasn't directed my way. The longer we've dated, though, the more that aspect of her personality has bled into our interactions, so I don't bother suggesting something for the meal tonight. I've never dated anyone so persistent about having things a certain way. Someone who can sometimes have a hard time going with the flow. Someone who is a tad uptight in the bedroom. Things are good there, but we're not rocking the bed and shattering glass with our screams. Shit, the one and only time I was with Palmer, we broke the bed and tore the curtains off the rod, and she almost ended up with a concussion.

I laugh to myself, remembering it even through the alcohol haze I had throughout.

But I tell myself that this is a mature relationship. Who cares if our sex isn't mind-blowing and out of this world? I still enjoy it and that's what matters.

"Hudson!" a group of kids scream.

I pocket my phone, heading over to the little people who make me feel like a rock star. My life is great, and I can't let Matt make me second-guess that. We're two very different people.

three

I sit in the booth next to my cousin Lance, staring between him and my other cousin Brinley. I don't understand how they think they can help. Lance is a businessman, and yes, he's worth millions, maybe even billions, but last I checked, he knows nothing about writing. And Brinley is now a tattoo artist. A super talented one, but she's not a writer.

"You could probably use some peace and a change of environment, right?" Lance asks, digging out his wallet and putting enough money on the table to cover more than what's been eaten. He glances over Brinley's shoulder and leans closer. "But Easton can't know, so just wait until he leaves, and we'll explain."

"Cryptic." Brinley laughs.

Easton returns from the bathroom, not bothering to sit back down. "I have to get going. I've got training at the sports complex. This is my year, I know it."

We all smile making it abundantly clear we're keeping something from him. He stares at us for a long moment, and we widen our smiles, making the situation even more awkward.

I wave and sign *good luck* while our other cousins say bye and huddle their heads in the middle of the table after Easton leaves.

"He knows we're keeping something from him," I say.

Brinley looks over her shoulder and shoos me with her hand. "I'll make something up if he asks."

Lance raises his wrist to check the time on his expensive watch. "We gotta go now because I have a meeting in an hour." He turns to Brinley. "Can you text Calista?"

"Why Calista?"

Brinley slides out of the booth. "You'll understand when we get there, but I'm supposed to open the shop, so we gotta go now."

"That's what I said." Lance hip-checks me to get me moving.

"Where are you taking me?" I ask.

She wraps her arm around me. "It's a surprise, but a great one. I promise."

We leave Lard Have Mercy, and since we all have to be places afterward, we each drive our own cars. Lance leads the way, heading toward the back part of Lake Starlight, where the lake isn't as deep and the houses are spread out from one another. The roads are narrow, causing me to grip the steering wheel tightly when another car comes from the opposite direction. I glance at the clock to see that there's plenty of time before I have to pick up Adley.

Eventually, they put on their turn signals, and I question what for until Lance pulls into a small driveway. When the trees clear, I see a little cottage tucked away in the forest. We barely fit all three cars on the gravel driveway, so when Calista drives up before I even get out of my car, she has to park sideways at the end to fit. I groan because I'm blocked in now. There's no fast getaway in my future.

"Hi!" she says, waving her hand with the heavy diamond ring. She opens her back door and grabs her four-year-old son, Jaden, from his car seat. He squirms to get down and runs toward us.

We each give him a high five, Brinley trying to snatch him up. Calista rounds the cars, and her swollen belly tucked under a maternity shirt is the first thing I notice about my eldest cousin.

"When did I miss this news?" I ask. "Where's Buzz Wheel when you need it?"

She laughs. "Then you definitely aren't keeping up with it. It was reported at, like, month three. I guess you show earlier with your second one." She rubs her belly, and the blush that fills her cheeks is completely envy-worthy.

I don't want to ever get married, but seeing some of my cousins—the three here right now—all settled down sometimes makes me wonder if maybe marriage could be for me someday. Especially when I see the glow on Calista's face. But I had that glow, too, when I was pregnant with Adley.

"And why isn't Mr. Jaden in preschool this morning?" Brinley asks, reluctantly letting him go since he refuses to be held.

"We leave for Chicago next week."

Calista's family spends their off months here, and during her husband Rylan's soccer season, they live in Chicago. She's told the family many times that once he retires, they'll be back in Lake Starlight for good, especially since her husband is from the Greene family in Sunrise Bay. At least she has Easton there in Chicago when it's baseball season.

"Already? That seemed short," Brinley says.

I get between them and raise my hands—I'm tired of talking today. *Why am I here in front of some creepy cottage in the middle of nowhere?*

They laugh. I'm fortunate that most of my family has learned how to sign. Although I can read lips, and with my cochlear implants, I can hear them, I still sign a lot of the time. When I was younger, I only communicated through sign language, and each of my cousins, aunts, and uncles took classes. I never take that for granted. Some are more fluent than others, but they can usually get the gist of what I'm saying if I don't sign too fast. If not, someone else translates for me.

"Come." Lance swings his arm around my shoulders, guiding me toward the house.

He passes a key to Calista, who uses it to open the cottage. We each walk through the cute, rounded door that has a small window on top. There's a sofa with a quilted afghan lying across the back and a kitchen with what appears to be the necessities in the far back corner.

"This was Great-Grandma Dori's hideaway," Lance says, taking the key back from Calista.

I turn in another circle, soaking up the space differently knowing it belonged to my great-grandma. I've always hated that Adley will never get to meet her. All of their eyes are on me.

I don't understand.

Brinley and Lance look at Calista. Meanwhile, Jaden is jumping on the couch. Calista digs her phone out of her coat pocket and puts him in the chair. Once he's settled, she returns to us.

"You weren't here, but do you remember when my friend Aubrey was getting married?" Calista asks.

I shrug.

"Yeah, it was when you were off exploring the world."

I roll my eyes.

"She was getting married, and Rylan returned to town to be Declan's best man, and I was the maid of honor. I hadn't seen him in so long—"

"Get on with it. I have to get going." Lance glances at his watch again.

"Anyway, Alice, Aubrey's grandma, brought me here, then a lawyer Great-Grandma Dori hired showed up and said the cabin was mine. He handed me a letter from her and a key. Told me I could do what I want with it, so I chose to keep it a secret from the family. Although I'll warn you, I think everyone's parents know about it, but I'm pretty sure they don't know which one of us is occupying it at any given time."

Lance blows out a frustrated breath.

Calista gives him a beseeching look. "She doesn't know any of this."

"Give her the short version." He sits in one of the kitchen chairs.

"When Brinley needed to get out of her apartment when Van first moved in, I gave the key to her. The lawyer guy left me the letters for each of our cousins, and so I gave her her letter." She digs into her purse and holds out a white envelope with my name scrolled across it in our great-grandma Dori's handwriting.

Air rushes from my lungs. I clutch the envelope hard and stare at it, unsure how to feel.

"Brinley gave the cabin to me when I returned to town with Kenzie, and she was supposed to marry that asshole," Lance says.

"It's supposed to be a place where you have some alone

time. Peace away from everything else. A place to find yourself. Find the right path," Brinley adds.

"When you said you couldn't concentrate, we thought maybe you could try to write here. Away from Adley and Hudson." Lance holds out the key.

"And when you're finished with it, if you find another one of our cousins who needs it, pass it along." Calista smiles, taking the phone away from Jaden and picking him up. "Now, I have to get back. Jaden is spending the day with Rylan's parents. The week before we head out is always the hardest. Especially with this one's due date being while we're gone."

I sign *Thank you* and hug her.

"You're welcome. I do hope you find what you're looking for here. And don't forget to read the letter."

"I will." I kiss Jaden's cheek, and he squirms to get away.

Brinley and Lance are quick to leave with smiles on their faces. After I back out of the driveway to let them get their cars out, and I return to the cottage, the door shuts, and I stand there in silence. I swear I can almost feel my great-grandma's arms around me. I walk around and admire the pictures of her and my great-grandpa, who I never met. The love between them shines bright in each one.

There's a small bedroom off the kitchen area and a bathroom, but that's it. The cottage is quaint and cute, and I can't believe my great-grandparents had a secret house. Well, actually, I can believe Great-Grandma Dori did. Maybe my great-grandpa was as secretive and spunky as her.

I sit on the couch, sinking so far down into the cushion that I fear I might not get up. Yeah, I could totally see myself writing here during the day, especially when Hudson has Adley. The more I imagine myself sitting at the small kitchen table or sitting on the couch or chair, I like the idea even more.

The envelope in my lap begs me to read it. The last words my great-grandma wrote to me are hidden away in that letter. The last advice from her I'll ever get because I know she wouldn't fill it with how proud she is of me. Guiding me to some end is more her style.

My finger runs along the top, and I pull out the paper perfectly folded in threes. Opening it, my heart swells when I see her writing fills the page. I read the first line.

My Dearest Palmer...

I drop the letter in my lap, not ready to read her last words. Quickly, I fold it back up and stuff it in the envelope, which I place on the coffee table. I'll spend time in her world first, this cottage, the place where she found refuge when life was crazy—or probably when she wanted to screw my great-grandpa. I have to push that mental image from my mind.

The alarm on my phone buzzes, reminding me it's time for me to grab Adley, so I rise from the couch and stare around the room before walking out and locking the cottage behind me. Tomorrow, after I drop off Adley at school, I'll come here, and maybe if I'm lucky, I won't have to call my editor and tell her I don't have a manuscript.

My phone dings as I climb into my SUV. It's my cousin, Harper.

> Did you know that Hudson is coaching Matt
> Peterson today?

> No. But they're friends from what I know.

He's in town, and if you want to finish that book of yours, maybe you should get on top of Matt for a night for inspiration. The man is GORGEOUS.

> Calm down there kitten. :P

Oh I don't want him. I overheard that he's having dinner at Hudson's tonight. Just do a drop by to see for yourself.

> I'm not really interested.

You will be. Report back on how he looks out of all that snowboarder gear.

I roll my eyes. My cousin is such a hornball.

> BYE Harper.

You're a buzzkill.

I drop my phone in the center console and back out of the driveway to head toward the school, but what Harper said echoes through my thoughts as I drive. Do I need to have sex to get me in the mood to write this book? And if so, Matt Peterson would be perfect. His reputation makes it clear he doesn't want anything serious, so it could be a one-and-done or maybe even a fling while he's here.

No. I don't need to sleep with a man in order to write a romance novel. Everyone knows book boyfriends are so much better than the real thing. What could a playboy snowboarder teach me? Nothing.

HUDSON

I pull into the driveway. My house is pitch black while Palmer's is flooded with light from almost every window. I swear she never worries about the electricity bill. I've been the one to teach Adley to turn off the lights after she's done in a room.

As always if I'm by myself, I veer toward Palmer's back door instead of going into my own house. I've never liked being alone. Up until we moved here, I always had roommates even when I didn't need one to share the rent. I'm a people person, and I find being alone lonely most times.

I open the door, and I'm surprised to find Palmer in the kitchen. She turns to me since she's wearing her cochlear implants and heard me. These days when she has Adley, she usually always has them on, so she can hear if anything happens when they aren't in the same room.

She raises her hands. *I heard about your new client.*

I roll my eyes. "Harper?"

Laughing, she stirs what looks like spaghetti sauce. It's one of Adley's favorites and an easy go-to when you've had a long day. I place my hands on her shoulders, massaging them. The stress and pressure of a book deadline always leaves her tight. She leans back into me, and I wrap my arms around her.

"You need a really good massage," I whisper.

She sets the spoon down and turns around. *Harper says I need to get laid.*

"That's what I said this morning. I'm not sure I like having the same thoughts as her."

Again, she giggles and moves to the oven, where she takes out garlic bread.

I have no idea what Theresa has planned, but I'd love to stay here. "Do you have meatballs too?"

Placing the hot cookie sheet on the empty spot on the stove, she smiles over her shoulder and shakes her head.

"What? Spaghetti but no meatballs?"

She removes the oven mitts. *Adley doesn't want them tonight.*

Sometimes I don't understand my little girl. "Speaking of Adley…"

Palmer inhales a deep breath and nods. *I know.*

"Kissing?"

Wanting to kiss.

I scowl at her. "Same thing."

Not really. You know I'll get the blame. Romance author, remember?

"That has nothing to do with it." I step out of the kitchen. "*Adley!*"

Do we have to do this now?

"I'm done with getting the phone calls. Where were you earlier that you couldn't answer your phone, and I had to be bothered at work?" I usually never give her shit, but I've gotten the call from the school the last four times, and it's getting embarrassing.

*Oh, you'll never believe it. My cousins gave me—*she stops talking and turns around to face the stove.

"What?"

Before I can pry it out of her, Adley runs into the room. "Daddy!"

I pick her up and place her on the counter, caging her in with my arms on either side of her. "I cannot believe we have to have this conversation again, but Holden wants to play at recess, not be chased by you and your friends." I sign at the same time as I speak. It's what Palmer and I have done since she was little to help her learn. It's amazing what little sponges young kids can be.

She huffs. "No, he doesn't, Daddy." She crosses her arms.

I glance over my shoulder at Palmer, who is hiding her amusement with a dishcloth in front of her mouth.

"Why do you think that? Has he told you he wants you to chase him?"

She swings her feet back and forth. She's changed out of her clothes into a leotard with fake princess high heel slippers. "I don't know if I like him now. He said his dad said I was a stage five clinger. What does that mean?"

"Stage five clinger?" I ask.

Palmer steps up to our daughter, her hands going a mile a minute.

"Mommy, slow down."

Adley might not be able to decipher everything her mother is saying, but I can, and let's say Mama Palmer is pissed.

Palmer taps me on the shoulder, and I turn fully in her direction. *I should handle this since you have plans. You go.*

"We're a team."

Okay, have at it. She puts her hand out as if I'm going to regret this.

"Adley, sweetie, you're three—"

She crosses her arms, and her eyebrows draw down. "I'm almost four."

"Okay, you're almost four, and there is plenty of time in the future for boys. Holden is one of many fish in the sea."

Adley leans away from me to look at Palmer over my shoulder. "Holden is a fish?"

"No, Holden isn't a fish. I'm just saying there are a lot of boys."

"I want Holden. His favorite animal is a gorilla like me."

"And there are other boys who like gorillas too," I say.

Adley stares at me. "So?"

I exhale a frustrated breath. "So, you can't go around chasing boys, okay? The boys will come to you, you don't have to go to them. When you're older."

"I should wait?" Adley asks.

A tap on my shoulder tells me I've fucked this up. I turn, and Palmer hip-checks me out of the way.

If you like a boy, there is no harm in telling him. But then you wait. Would you like it if one of your other friends chased you?

"NO!"

Exactly. If Holden likes you, he'll come to you. She pokes Adley in the stomach and Adley laughs. *Spaghetti time?*

"Yay!" Adley raises her hands in the air.

So, you aren't going to chase Holden anymore, right?

She shakes her head, sending her brown hair flicking side to side. "No chasing."

I have my suspicions that this will continue, but hopefully Palmer got through to her. I hear a vehicle outside and look out the window to see Theresa pull up behind my truck in my driveway.

"I gotta go. Have a good night, ladies." I pretend to bow as though I'm a prince.

Adley laughs, hugging me, then I get her off the counter, set her on her feet, and twirl her around with my finger in her hand. The ruffled flare of the leotard spins.

"Bye!"

Palmer waves, busy getting Adley's plate ready.

I head outside to cross the two driveways, a path worn in the snow from us going back and forth to each other's places. Theresa's head is in the trunk of her small SUV, and I go around to help her. She has three bags, and all I see are the plastic bags from the produce section. Of course she's picked something healthy.

"Over at Palmer's again?"

There isn't any disdain in her voice. Theresa's known from day one how close Palmer and I are and that we're committed to parenting together. She doesn't have the same relationship with her ex—they still meet at a public place to exchange their daughter. He lives over in Winter-berry Falls.

"Yeah, got another call from the school today about Adley and this Holden kid."

"I understand the concern as a teacher, but they are only three."

I unlock the side door of the house and allow her to go first.

"I think Palmer got through to her. Hopefully." I put the bags down on the kitchen counter and pull out the items.

"Do you think it's because of Palmer and the romance writer thing?"

"Given the fact that Adley can barely read, I'd say no."

I'm a bit irritated that she said that—especially since that's exactly what Palmer was worried about.

"I just mean Palmer probably talks about her stories with the people in her life. Maybe Adley overheard her talking about kissing and—"

"Yeah, I'm not sure, but I doubt it."

"Okay. I was just thinking out loud."

"Can we drop it?" I take the plastic bags and put them in the container I keep them in in the laundry room.

"Of course."

"What are you making?" I ask, wanting to change the subject.

"Stir fry with tofu," she says. "Hope you're ready to chop."

Because we're both on edge after she blamed Palmer's job for the reason Adley's chasing a boy around the playground, I don't groan and complain like I usually would when she picks tofu instead of meat. I'll suck it up and eat a bowl of cereal later tonight. Besides, she's doing me a solid by even making this dinner.

I nod. "Sounds good."

"Great, you chop, and I'll make the sauce and rice."

I sit at the table with a cutting board and the vegetables. She grabs her apron from one of the drawers. She leaves one here now because the first time she cooked, and I didn't have one, her blouse got ruined. She looks cute in it, all put together in a perfect little package.

"So, how was your day?" I ask, using my phone to turn on the stereo for background noise.

She talks about a boy in her class who has been giving her trouble. I'm familiar with the name and other problems he has caused for her this year. After she sets the rice to cook, she goes into my family room and straightens up, coming back with a cup Adley was using last night and an empty bowl from the popcorn we ate while watching a movie.

"You've got to start cleaning up unless you want Adley to be a slob when she grows up." She holds up the two items.

To stop a fight from starting, I nod and smile. "It was late by the time the movie ended, and this morning was crazy when you came with breakfast."

She turns from the stove. "Would you rather I not surprise you with breakfast?"

"No."

"Is it an inconvenience?"

"No, I just meant we have a routine, and maybe that cup and bowl would've been picked up had you not surprised me." I chop the green pepper and put it aside. At this point, I'm wishing I would've met Matt at a fucking bar.

"Doubtful, but nice thinking."

My hand tightens on the handle of the knife. Thankfully, the doorbell rings, so I stand to answer it. Matt must have taken an Uber because a car pulls away from the curb the minute I open the door.

"Hey, man." I shake his hand and open the door wider for him.

"Thanks for having me." He holds up a bottle of wine and a six-pack. "Not sure which you prefer."

"Theresa can have the wine, and we can split the beer." I take both from his hands.

A throat clears, and we both turn our attention to Theresa standing in the entrance to the kitchen.

"Matt, this is Theresa."

"The little woman," he says, and I inwardly groan.

"Little woman? Where did you just warp in from?" she asks.

Matt laughs. "I'm just joking. Nice to meet you. Where is the little woman, though?" He shakes Theresa's hand.

Theresa looks at me with an arched eyebrow.

"Adley is at her mom's." I point in the direction of Palmer's house.

"She lives next door?" Matt asks.

"They have an unorthodox relationship," Theresa says. She takes the bottle of wine and the six-pack from me. "I'll get you a glass for that beer."

Matt stares at her ass and turns back to me, giving me his appreciation for her. Theresa is good-looking, but I doubt she's the kind of woman Matt has ever been with. "I don't need a glass. Bottle is fine."

By the time we make it into the kitchen, she's already pouring it. "It's no problem."

"What's for dinner?" Matt peers into the wok Theresa has on the stove.

I sit back down to cut the remaining vegetables.

"Stir fry with tofu." Theresa smiles and turns back to the stove.

"Yum," Matt says, eyes widening as he joins me at the table.

Dinner goes well, Theresa seeming impressed by Matt and his accomplishments. She pulls out a cake from a bag on the counter that I didn't realize she'd brought and opens up the freezer, her shoulders sagging.

"What?" I ask.

"You don't have ice cream?"

"Sorry, last night was sundae night with Adley. We used it all up. I'm sure just the cake is good."

"It's supposed to be served with ice cream," Theresa says.

I'm thinking I've caught her on a bad day because we both seem irritable with each other. This has never really happened before between us, and when she excuses herself for the bathroom, Matt is quick to jump on it.

"She's wound...tight," he says.

"I think she had a bad day. I'll be right back. I'm going to get some ice cream from Palmer's." I leave my house and go to Palmer's, but the back door is locked, so I have to knock.

Adley runs up, freshly bathed and in her Wonder Woman flannel pajama set. Palmer comes right after her, still dressed in jeans and sweater. She helps Adley open the door.

"Hi, Daddy!"

"Do you have ice cream?" I pick up Adley and walk in, shutting the door to not let in the cold air.

"Ice cream?" Adley's eyes light up.

Palmer nods.

"Theresa brought cake for dessert, but Adley and I ate all mine yesterday."

Palmer digs into her freezer and pulls out a new container. Adley is addicted to ice cream and likes to make her own sundaes. "Here you go."

"Thanks."

"I want cake!" Adley grins at me.

Is Matt over there? Palmer glances out her kitchen window.

"I want cake!" Adley says again—to Palmer this time.

Ask Daddy, if he says yes then...

I give Palmer the evil eye because she's backed me into a

corner, and she knows it. Theresa and I are already not on the same page tonight. Bringing Palmer over won't help anything, but I'm not going to just bring Adley over—it feels rude.

We'll be quick.

"Yes. Quick like bunnies." Adley and Palmer both put on their best smiles.

"Fine. Let's go. But cake, and then it's your bedtime. Got it?"

Adley nods. "Got it."

We put on Adley's coat, and I walk with them over to my house. I can't wait to see Theresa's reaction. Hopefully this doesn't make things even worse, but I suspect I already know the answer to that.

HUDSON

I open the door, Theresa's laugh billowing out of the kitchen from some joke that Matt probably told her. The guy can be hilarious when he's not too crude for someone like Theresa.

Am I really that different from when we used to hang together? I get the domesticated thing, settling roots and being a dad, but I didn't think my personality had changed that much. But I even cringed at a few of the things Matt said during dinner.

Matt smiles over Theresa's shoulder when we enter the kitchen.

"Found ice cream," I say, raising it.

"Oh good." Theresa pushes up from the table and turns, stopping when she sees Palmer and Adley with me. "Oh, and you brought extras."

I hope that's okay. Sorry for interrupting.

I translate Palmer's sign language for Theresa.

"Of course. There's plenty." She puts on a fake-ass smile that I'm sure even Matt can see through, and he doesn't even know her.

"Palmer?" Matt says, rising to his feet from the table. "Nice to meet you." He signs.

She blinks for a beat along with me. *You know how to sign?*

"A little." He continues to sign as he speaks, missing a few words, but overall doing okay. "In high school, I had the option to take sign language or Spanish, and I already knew I sucked at Spanish, so I gave sign language a shot."

This is Adley. Palmer puts her hand on our daughter's back.

Matt crouches down to her level, putting his hand up in the air. "Give me five."

Adley smacks it like she does with her uncles, harder than most three-year-olds.

"Whoa." He shakes out his hand.

Palmer laughs, and I glance at her, wondering where that flirtatious sound came from. I guess it's been a while since I've been around Palmer and a man who wasn't someone she's related to. She got pregnant and wasn't interested in sex, then after Adley was born, she always said how disgusting she felt. At some point last year, Palmer went on a girls' trip with some of her cousins, and from listening to their cryptic talk, I think maybe Palmer hooked up with someone, but I wasn't there to see it.

"I like her already. Teaching her how to inflict pain."

The two of them laugh, and Matt steps aside, pulling a chair out for Adley first then Palmer.

"I wish you would've told me they were coming," Theresa whispers while cutting the cake.

"It was a spur-of-the-moment thing," I whisper back.

"It's just that I wanted to get to know your friend, and now…"

"What?" I stop scooping the ice cream and stare at her.

"Nothing. Let's just get this over with." She takes two bowls over to the table and passes them out, adding a sweetness to her tone I only ever hear when she's hiding something.

"Palmer says it looks delicious," Matt translates since both of our backs are facing them.

A growl stops short from erupting up my throat.

Theresa turns away from the counter and smiles. "Thank you."

"Chocolate is my favorite," Adley says, using her spoon to dig into the cake.

As Adley eats her cake and ice cream, Matt and Palmer continue to chat using sign language.

So, why did you pick Hudson to train you?

Matt thinks for a moment before signing. *We were friends before you came into his life. Even though he's a pussy now, he knows the sport better than anyone else.*

Palmer is quick to respond. *Are you suggesting I took him away from something?*

Matt shakes his head. *No. He could still be out there doing tricks.*

I hit Matt's arm to gain his attention. *I told you, I'm happy. Leave it.*

"Could you translate?" Theresa asks me. "I feel like the odd man out."

"I don't know either." Adley piles another spoonful in her mouth. She's learned a lot of sign language quickly, but when the hands move too fast, she can't follow.

"Then I guess we can have our own conversation." Theresa elbows Adley and laughs.

Palmer stares at Theresa for a beat and inhales a sharp

breath. I'm sure she's annoyed about what Theresa said, having no idea what it was like for Palmer growing up and even now with her implants. Theresa's comment was insensitive.

Palmer's gaze lands on me, and she nods toward Theresa. *Tell her I'm sorry.*

I shake my head.

Tell her.

No, it won't do any good. Just carry on.

Matt's spoon drops into his bowl, and he signs. *Do you two fight like you're a couple?*

We both turn to him. *No,* we sign in unison.

Matt laughs.

"What's so funny?" Theresa looks between us all.

"Just these two. They must give you comic relief."

"Yeah, all the time." Her tone is sarcastic, and the table grows quiet for a beat.

Palmer quickly finishes her cake and ice cream, urging Adley to finish hers. *Come on, it's almost bedtime.*

Matt touches Palmer's arm, and she turns in his direction, a smile already on her face. *You're leaving so soon?*

She needs to go to bed.

"I'm not tired," Adley says.

"You will be when your head hits the pillow," I tell her.

"No, I won't."

"Yes, you will," I say.

Adley scoops up a small amount of ice cream, taking her time eating it.

This is like dinner and a show.

Palmer laughs at Matt's quip and signs back to him. *You should see the two of them fight over the television.*

I lift my hands to join the conversation. *Maybe if you*

sided with me more often, she wouldn't think she could fight back with me. I am her father.

Matt's jaw drops. *Whoa, you sounded like my dad there. Scary.*

Shut up. I sign, growing more annoyed.

Come on. Palmer puts her hand on Adley's arm. *You can take it home with you.*

Palmer stands and picks up Adley, who's fussing as if she doesn't want to leave. Matt gets up from his chair, and I narrow my eyes, wondering what the hell he's doing. Surely he understands that Palmer is mine. Well, not mine, but there's no room for him in our situation. She's my daughter's mother, which means he needs to find someone else to fuck around with while he's in town.

I'll walk you back, Matt signs.

Palmer smiles and points toward her house. *We're right next door. I'll be fine.*

Who is going to hold her ice cream?

She stares at him for a moment and nods.

I kiss Adley goodbye, and her small arms tighten around my neck. God, I love her so much. She's worth every day that I don't do a stupid trick on the halfpipe. The three leave, and I watch through the window as they make their way over to Palmer's house. Palmer slips, and Matt steadies her, almost dropping the ice cream, but of course, he saves the day.

"Are you going to stand there all night?" Theresa asks from the kitchen.

As I turn my head in her direction, Matt walks into Palmer's house.

What the fuck is going on?

"Jesus, Hudson, what am I missing?"

Stripping myself away from the window, I join Theresa

as she cleans up, packaging the leftovers that she's more than welcome to take home.

I don't respond because I've never felt whatever this is stirring inside me. I've never felt this feeling that's brewing under my usual casual demeanor. Matt is a friend, and Palmer isn't looking for anything serious. Why not let her have some fun while he's in town? But something inside me doesn't like it.

"Hudson!" Theresa says louder.

"What?" I run my hand through my hair, pulling on the back of my neck. "I just don't want Matt to use Palmer."

She scoffs. "From what I hear, it'd be the other way around." She puts the lid on the ice cream, and I'm tempted to return it right now to interrupt the two of them next door.

"What's that mean?"

She turns around and puts her hands on the counter on either side of her. "I've heard rumors about that girls' trip she took with her cousins. That she was looking hard to hook up with someone, and that she was with different people every night."

Irritation sparks like a match in my chest. I could see her meeting one guy and spending the trip with him, but she's never been the type to hop from guy to guy. "That's not Palmer."

"Of course you defend her. That's the reason I never told you." She puts the leftovers in her bag. Good, because I wasn't going to eat them.

"First of all, I don't need to defend her because even if it were true, she was single and could do who and what she wanted. Regardless, rumors are rarely true."

She huffs and shakes her head. "Am I in the middle of something I shouldn't be?"

"What do you mean?" I grab a washcloth and wipe down the table, especially where Adley was.

"You know what I mean. Do you have feelings for Palmer?"

"I love Palmer, but I'm not *in* love with her. She's my best friend and the mother—"

"Of your daughter. I get it. That's what you always say, but the man I saw tonight wanted to reach across that table and rip Matt's head off for flirting with his best friend." Her eyebrows rise, asking me to answer to my reaction that I haven't even deciphered yet.

"It's just me being protective. That's all. We have a good thing going with co-parenting Adley, and I don't want anything to disturb that." I start on the dishes, wishing we could end this conversation.

"And where does that leave me?" She grabs a dish towel.

I hand her a pot once I'm finished washing it. "You're my girlfriend—I don't understand what you're asking."

"How far can we go? Because from where I sit, the merging of our lives is already causing a disturbance for me."

"For you?" I laugh. "How are you disturbed by my relationship with my daughter and her mother?"

The pot slips from her hands and clatters to the floor. We both reach down to pick it up. "Sometimes I don't know if it's ignorance or stupidity with you."

We both stand, and I stare at her for a moment, wondering where the woman from this morning is. "Spit out what you really want to say, Theresa."

She puts the pot on the counter with the dish towel. "Tonight was about us having your friend over. And as long as you live next door to her, we'll never be able to be a real couple."

"They just came over for dessert."

"And you've been distracted since they arrived."

"I borrowed their ice cream. It would be rude not to let them have some cake." Maybe it's a weak excuse, but whatever.

"You could have gone to the grocery store. You didn't have to go next door and borrow it."

I scrunch my eyebrows because that makes no sense. "But—"

"See! I wanted to feel like a real couple tonight, where we entertain your friend, and I hear stories about your youth and all the stupid things you did. But instead, I got to sit at a table not understanding what you guys were saying because you were all signing."

"I apologize. I should have done a better job filling you in, but that was only at the end of the night, Theresa. The rest of the dinner went great."

She's quiet, and for the first time with her, I'm not sure how to react. We've never had a conversation with this much honesty, at least on her part. Where do we go from here?

"I just always feel...lacking with her. Like you wish..."

"Hey." I place my hands on her hips and pull her toward me. "Palmer and I had our moment, and we decided to remain friends and raise our daughter together. It's the reason we live close but separate. If there was anything there, I wouldn't be standing here with you. I'm not that type of guy."

She looks up at me. "Really?"

"Yes. I want you here and in my life."

Her arms slide around my middle, and she steps into

me. I tighten my grip on her, and she sighs against my chest.

I look over her head at Palmer's house, watching her shut the blinds to the window that faces my house. I inhale a breath and kiss Theresa on the head.

I like Theresa. A lot, but fuck, I'm pretty sure I just lied to her.

PALMER

Idrop off Adley at preschool, reminding her again to keep her hands to herself and not to chase Holden around the playground. She agrees, but she's done that before.

Driving over to the cottage with my laptop, I can't stop thinking about last night. Matt waited downstairs for me to get Adley to sleep, then we talked for about an hour before I was yawning, and he said he should go. My excitement is too much to contain, and the minute I get into the cottage, I text my cousin Harper, who I wish I could just have come over here, but rules are rules, and I'm not supposed to tell anyone else about this place.

> So, I met Matt Peterson last night…

Three dots appear immediately.

> Don't hold back the details! How was it?!?

> Adley was home.

(girl throwing tantrum GIF)

He's really cool, though. You'd never know he's an Olympian. He just seems like a regular guy.

You mean a hot AF regular guy. His name was being said all over the slopes yesterday. I'm sure more people will be there today expecting him.

Yeah, more women. Women who know how to ski and snowboard.

I should've allowed my family to teach me when I was younger, but even though I liked adventure, I wasn't the outdoorsy type of girl. I was the "stay by the fire in the lodge" type of girl. I saw Matt's disappointment when he asked me last night whether I could ski or snowboard.

You know I'll teach you.

Yeah, Hudson's been begging me to go out with him and Adley.

Your daughter is a mean snowboarder for only being almost four.

She'd put me to shame. LOL

Where are you? Let's meet up for lunch or something.

I have Adley with me. I'm trying to finish this book for my editor who is going to call me tomorrow to see how it's going.

I don't like lying to her, but I can't tell her where I am.

What's the hang-up?

It's just not coming to me.

Oh…right about a one-night stand. I always love those stories.

Isn't that your parents' story? I've heard about the Jeep.

(a girl throwing up GIF) I do not speak about your parents' extracurriculars, and you do not speak about mine.

I'm just saying, they were hot gossip around this town once upon a time.

There's your story. Hot snowboarder comes to small town and falls madly in love with a single mom.

And where's the conflict?

The best friend slash baby daddy wants her too.

HARPER! Stop it.

I can almost hear her laughing.

(laughing girl GIF) It'll be written on my gravestone that Hudson loves Palmer.

She's always been so hung up on us, even though I've explained a million times that Hudson and I were a one-and-done.

Hate to break your heart, but Hudson's with Theresa and things are getting serious.

Lately I've realized how much one of us meeting someone we're serious about can change our family dynamic. It scares me. I felt the tension radiating off Theresa last night and with good reason. Adley and I bulldozed our way in there, and that was unfair. Maybe we need to set some boundaries. Boundaries have never been an issue before, but maybe this is just the reality of how things need to be.

He'll break up with her before they get that serious, you watch.

She seems to make him happy.

Not as happy as you.

I open my laptop, staring at my blank screen, then I glance at the time on the top right corner.

OK I gotta go write this book. Thanks for the distraction.

Happy to be a distraction. We need to get together soon.

I'll text you.

Remember, a hot snowboarder is a great hero.

Bye, Harper!

(laughing girl GIF)

I put my phone on vibrate and shove it under my leg, turning off my cochlear implants. I close my eyes, inhaling and exhaling, trying to ignite something in my mind, some spark of inspiration.

My fingers start typing without me looking at the screen.

He's the hot up-and-coming Olympic snowboarder, and she's the reserved single mom. Both are only looking for one thing...

I open my eyes and read the paragraph I wrote, but something feels off. So I grab a notebook from my bag, hoping to sketch out the storyline, see how far I can get it.

I use my usual methods, writing everything and anything that could happen. All the what-if scenarios. I can't believe Harper got me on this line of thinking. I mean, Matt was great, but he's not the "hero of a love story" kind of guy. He's the guy who broke the girl's heart, so the hero has to mend it and make it whole again.

I press the delete key until I'm back to a blank page.

Blowing out a breath, I think about all the tropes I love. Those are always easier to write.

When nothing helps, I shut my laptop, toss it on the adjacent chair, and walk around the small space, hoping Great-Grandma Dori channels something inside me that will help.

I open drawers and cabinets, not finding much except evidence that Rylan and Calista spent some time here. There's some Wok For U chopsticks and fortune cookies in a drawer with takeout menus. They love the orange chicken like most of the Bailey clan, but they practically live there during Rylan's off-season, saying they've never found any better Chinese takeout than here in Lake Starlight.

The bedroom is small, with only room for a bed and a dresser. The dresser drawers are all empty, but the closet has poster boards in one corner, slides in another. Being nosy, I go through them and laugh.

Each board is Great-Grandma Dori's mission board on how to get one of my aunts or uncles together with who she thought was the love of their life. I dig deep into the back and find my own parents' board. Front and center is a picture of me at only eighteen months.

Sedona and Jamison

Palmer needs her daddy.

It goes through all the steps to help push my parents together. A story I learned as a teenager that made me loathe my parents for keeping it from me all those years. Ultimately, I understood as I got older that relationships are complicated. Especially, since I returned to Lake Starlight much like my mom did—pregnant. The only difference was that my baby daddy was with me, whereas my mom was alone.

Great-Grandma Dori sure went to a lot of work, but her and her best friend Ethel's planning was flawless. Everything is detailed, all the way down to what they expect will happen to break them up—or what I call the black moment in my books. I wonder who she would've seen for me and what her plan would have been. There's a sad tug on my heart that I'll never know.

Of course, it would probably be Hudson. Everyone in this town thinks Hudson and I are stupid because we should be a couple. As if it's that easy to be a couple. Not to mention, I'm not looking for a forever man. I like my life the way it is, and if Hudson and I got together and things went south, there's no way we could still have the easy co-parenting relationship we do now.

I head back to the couch, my head as bleak as it was before my walk around the cabin. Lying down and pulling the afghan over me, I set my alarm on my phone for twenty minutes and shove it under the pillow. A quick nap will hopefully refresh me.

Twenty minutes later, my head vibrates from my phone, and I reach under the pillow to grab it, turning it off. I close my eyes briefly and recall the most vivid dream I just had. Grabbing my laptop, I can't open my blank file fast enough.

My fingers land on the keyboard with a thud and move on their own accord.

Bea was quiet, reserved. She wasn't like her roommate, Nia, who drew the attention of all the boys. Bea was plus size, large-framed, big-boned, whichever word was politically correct these days. Nia was slim, fit, and could make any piece of clothing look good.

Nia walked into the small mountain bar where she was supposed to meet up with some drummer. She'd asked Bea to join her just in case things went south. Bea already knew what to expect from the night. She'd be nursing a drink at the bar while Nia flitted around, flirting and holding court. But she had no other plans for the night, so Bea had agreed to come anyway.

They had no sooner gotten their drinks than the drummer (Trek, Trey, Trev?) approached Nia from behind. He covered her eyes and looked at Bea, smiling wide. He was cute in that rock star type of way—messy dark hair that looked on the verge of greasy with a band T-shirt she didn't think was his actual band, along with a pair of jeans and metal chain that went from his belt loop to his wallet. And of course, the finishing touch—a pair of beat-up Converse. He was Nia's type, which assured Bea that her assumption was correct. Bea would nurse a drink until Nia told her she was going home with him, then all three of them would take an Uber to their place and she'd be rewarded with having an awkward run-in with him in the kitchen in the morning. If Bea was really lucky, she'd bump into him in the middle of the night in the hallway after he used the bathroom, and of course, he wouldn't have put the toilet seat back down.

"Guess who?" he says.

What are we, five? *Bea thought and quickly reprimanded herself. The reason she didn't have a boyfriend was because of intrusive thoughts like that. She could be a tad judgmental and nit-picked any guys who hit on her.*

"I could tell those calluses anywhere," Nia said and turned around and hugged Trek—at least Bea thought that was his name.

Bea refrained from calling Nia on her bullshit since she liked anyone who played in a band, especially a drummer, and everyone knew they had calluses. Again, Bea assumed this was why she couldn't find anyone. She refused to act like one of those stupid giddy girls. Flirting was not Bea's forte.

"Let me show you the set list," the drummer said.

Nia glanced at Bea as if Bea might say no, stay here. Bea had never said no, stay here. She waved her friend to go on, encouraging like any good wingwoman should. Nia slid off her stool and accepted his hand, and he dragged her away as she laughed at some stupid joke he'd made.

Bea raised her hand to the bartender. When she went to bars with live bands, she relied on reading lips and pointing most of the time to get what she wanted. Most of the time, no one was the wiser that she was deaf. Most people would be amazed how much you don't have to talk in a bar. Hell, she'd gotten away with actually sleeping with a guy once without him knowing she was deaf. But Bea had always felt misunderstood, and sometimes it was easier to avoid the whole thing altogether.

The bartender had messy sandy-blond hair that looked thick and luscious. He had light eyes. Bea couldn't quite tell whether they were green or blue or a mix of both in the dim lighting, but they held kindness when he approached her.

"What can I get you?" he asked, leaning closer so she could see a light five o'clock shadow that made him look even sexier.

She pointed at the beer the guy had next to her. The bartender nodded and opened a cooler with the bottom of his shirt that gave Bea a glimpse of his happy trail.

"My name is Pete. Holler if you need something." He smiled, and Bea's stomach erupted into butterflies.

Maybe this evening wouldn't be a bust after all.

My fingers stop, and I break into a big smile. Finally, the writing gods are with me again. I feel the energy inside my bones, the excitement brewing in my stomach—this is the story I'm meant to write.

seven

HUDSON

Matt texted that he'd be waiting up by the halfpipe for me rather than meeting me in the lodge. Which means one of two things. One, he isn't looking to hook up with anyone, and his mind is only on snowboarding. Or two, he already knows who he wants to hook up with.

I take my board to meet him, and I'm not surprised when I arrive, and a bunch of locals are cheering him on as he does his run. Probably half the reason he wanted to come here is for an ego boost. I'm sure it works—if people thinking you're a big deal makes you think you are too.

I rest my board in the snow and sit, waiting for him to come back up. I missed his first two tricks, but all the locals can't stop saying how awesome he was.

"Remember, he's been doing this a long time. Don't attempt any stupid shit," I remind them since a lot of them here are novices.

"Such a buzzkill, Hudson. We're not stupid."

I nod. "Well, I just wanted to say it in case anyone was feeling adventurous."

When Matt gets back to the top of the mountain, he smacks hands and smiles at their praises. One thing I've wondered about over the past few years is whether I would be as fearless as he is. You have to be in order to be successful in this profession. I tell myself I quit because of Adley, but it could be I never had the guts.

Matt plops down beside me. "What did you think?"

"I missed the first two tricks, but you got a lot of height on that last one."

"Yeah, I've got an extra pep in my step today. If I could've come out here last night after dinner, I would've…" He picks up some snow and tosses it in the air.

"Tofu stir fry or chocolate cake does it for you?"

"More like a cute brunette."

My gut twists. I should've known.

"Adley? I know she's cute, right? She's got my blood, so what did you expect?" I laugh, but Matt stares at me because he obviously wants to have this conversation.

This isn't the first time I've had to have the "are you sure" conversation with a friend. My only problem with Matt is that I know he's not looking for anything more than sex, and Palmer says the same, but I worry about her getting hurt.

"Go ahead," I say, not wanting to delay this any further.

"Is there something between you two?" Matt asks, staring me in the eye.

Although I don't spend a lot of time with Matt anymore, I know him, and he would never cross the line if I asked him not to. I could be honest and say that I didn't like seeing the two of them together. So much so, it caused a fight with Theresa.

My phone buzzes in my pocket. "Hold on."

Pulling it out of my pocket, I take off my glove and put

in my password. It's from Palmer.

> Holy shit! I just had the best writing day I've had in over a year. Maybe it's Matt like you said. I forgot how good it feels.

> Anyway, see you in a couple hours. Going to get some writing in during her nap time.

> That's awesome! I knew it would come eventually. You'll have to tell me about it when you drop Adley off.

There's no answer, which doesn't surprise me because that's Palmer. When the words are flowing, she goes into her writing cave, only poking her head out occasionally.

"Theresa?" Matt asks.

I pocket my phone and put my glove back on. "Palmer. She had a good writing day today."

Matt smiles. "That's good. She told me she was going to call her editor today and accept defeat."

I nod. "Guess not anymore. Anyway, it's fine. You can ask her out. She's Adley's mom, and we're best friends, but that's where it ends for us. We've never been romantically involved, except for the night we conceived Adley."

"So, I can pursue her?"

I laugh and give him one long stare. "Ask her out on a date?"

"She's your baby mama. I'm not gonna disrespect her."

My eyebrows lift. "I'll warn you that she might want you to disrespect her a little."

He sits up. "Is that your way of telling me she's kinky? What should I know about?"

I push him on the shoulder. "I meant that she's not really a relationship girl."

"All the better. But I really wanted to check with you first because last night you looked…"

"What?" I ask, my gaze straying to the halfpipe where some kid just fell on his ass after he came down from a trick.

"Jealous? Like we were leaving you out. Then again, Theresa is a bit…uptight?"

At least he's giving me the out to say it's Theresa and not him and Palmer until I can get a handle on whatever these feelings are I'm having. "She's particular, yeah."

"Does she not like Palmer?"

I shrug. "I think she's wary. She and her ex don't have a relationship like me and Palmer."

"You mean they aren't this century's version of the Cleavers?" He tosses snow at me.

I shake my head, picking up some snow and throwing it back at him. "I get that it's unusual, but if we're both cool with it, why do other people find it weird?"

He shrugs. "Something tells me Theresa likes control, and she can't control your situation."

"Yeah, maybe. She mentioned that it bothered her that I'm right next door to Palmer, but I'm never moving. It's too convenient living right next to Adley. It's as close as I can be in her life without actually living with her."

He nods and gets up on his board with one foot strapped in, then he moves to get in line for the halfpipe. "I think you might want to prepare yourself for a bumpy road, because you and Palmer can't live like you are forever. Most women would struggle with it. In all seriousness, if I was into Palmer, and let's say I wanted to marry her, it would probably feel like I'm marrying you too, and I wouldn't be cool with it."

As always, he makes his way to the front of the line. I try

to concentrate on his run. It's the reason he's here and the reason he's paying me, but all I can think about is whether he's right. Our situation is unconventional and not everyone in our lives is going to like it. The question is, do I give a shit? Which would mean how much do I care about Theresa? Enough to overhaul my entire life? I'm not so sure.

***

AFTER MATT and I spend the majority of the day working on his height and landings, we head back down the mountain. I'm meeting Palmer for Adley's weekly lesson and some ski time with my little girl. He's probably coming down the mountain with me to get Palmer to sleep with him while I'm with Adley, but he told me he just had to take a break.

Palmer is already at the fence line with Adley all bundled up and her board resting on the wooden divider between the skiers and non-skiers.

"She said she doesn't board?" Matt asks as we approach.

"Palmer?" I laugh. "No. Been trying to get her to for years."

"Huh."

"Ready?" I ask when we approach, but I can already tell from Adley's face that she's not happy to be here.

Palmer puts her hand on Adley's head and signs *Someone woke up from their nap cranky.*

I bend down to talk to my daughter, but the first thing I hear is "Hey, beautiful," from Matt to Palmer. I glance up and see Palmer's cheeks flush and not from the cold weather. Her dark hair is down, and she's got on a knit cap. Her lips are pink and rosy.

She waves and smiles at him.

I turn my attention to Adley because I can't keep fixating on them. I poke her in the stomach although her big jacket might make it so she can't feel it. "Come on, do you not want to go snowboarding with me today?"

"I'm tired," she whines and walks into my arms.

I hold her tightly, my hand running down her back. "How about we take it slow? We'll do a few runs, and if you don't wake up a bit by then, we'll call it a day and get hot cocoa in the lodge?"

She pulls back from me, and her small smile makes my heart grow larger.

"Okay?" I ask since she didn't answer.

She nods. "'Kay."

"Say goodbye to Mommy."

She walks over to Palmer and hugs her leg.

"I'll bring her home after."

"Does that mean you're free?" Matt asks Palmer.

"Um..." she says, and I'm surprised because she rarely speaks out loud around people she's not close to.

"I thought the book was pouring out of you. You should go write," I say.

Matt gives me a look as though I'm the worst wingman ever. "One drink in the lodge."

She looks at me as if she needs permission.

I hold up my hands. "Don't look at me. Your conscience will make the decision."

She rolls her eyes and turns to Matt, nodding. "Sure."

I have no idea why it irritates me so much that she feels comfortable enough to speak out loud with him.

"Great. Let me lock up my equipment, and I'll meet you in the lodge." He turns back to me. "Have fun shredding."

Matt holds his hand out for Adley to give him a high

five, but she curls into me more as if she doesn't remember him from last night. Her snubbing him shouldn't make me as happy as it does.

"Have fun, you two. We're out." I pick up Adley's board and mine.

We make our way to the bunny hill. One day soon, I want to get Adley up on one of the bigger hills just to test her out. She's capable. Most people think it's crazy to start a kid snowboarding so young, but most little ones are actually really good at it. And believe it or not, in some ways, it's way easier than teaching an adult beginner.

As we get to the top of the bunny hill, my phone vibrates in my pocket. I sit Adley down on the ground, her board strapped to her feet, and take off my gloves to see who it is.

Theresa: I want to make last night up to you. I'm sorry for the way I acted.

MY HEAD ROCKS BACK. I don't really want to get into this right now.

My gaze goes to the bottom of the hill where I can see the lodge entrance, and sure enough, Matt is walking through the doors.

Me: No apologies. How about we do movie night tonight?

Theresa: Can we do it at my place?

> Me: Sure, but I'll have to leave early because it's my turn to take Adley to preschool in the morning.

THE THREE DOTS appear then disappear. I wait a few minutes but assume she got distracted by her classroom of students or another teacher. I pocket the phone, get Adley up on her feet, and we snowboard down the bunny hill.

As I figured, after a few runs, Adley's excited and doesn't want to stop, so we continue until the lights turn on.

"Hot chocolate?" I ask after we finish the last run of the day.

She claps her mittens together. "Yes!"

I walk to the lodge and put our boards on the outside storage rack, thinking it won't take too long. As soon as I carry Adley inside, I hear the giggle that's been drilled into my head for years, and I turn toward the big leather chairs by the fire.

"Mommy!" Adley points at where Palmer and Matt are sitting, each having a drink and what looks like appetizers.

I lower Adley to the floor, and she runs over to Palmer, climbing into the seat with her, eager to tell her how well she did on the slopes. Matt turns to me. I nod and head to the bar to get our hot cocoa, then I join them, interrupting their time together. Oops.

Yeah, I really need to address whatever is going on inside me every time I see them alone together. But I'm just not ready yet.

eight

PALMER

Pete was slammed with customers while the band played. The music was okay, but it wasn't really his taste. There was more screaming and slamming on the cymbals than he preferred. But he'd deal with it in order to snowboard on the slopes all day and work at night.

After high school, he'd opted to go out and explore the world, much to his parents' displeasure, citing that he should go to college and find a career. Settle down with a wife and kids someday. That wasn't Pete's thing. Snowboarding was his one true love. His goal was to board every big ski resort in the mountains, maybe make it in the competitive world. He'd headed west after graduating from a small high school in Vermont. Now, he found himself in Oregon. He should have been preparing to leave here, but something had kept him from making plans to do so, and he couldn't put a finger on why.

At the moment, he couldn't keep his eyes off the curvy brunette nursing beers at the end of the bar. He had been flirting with her between delivering drinks until he and Dimitri ended up switching sides, and now all Pete could do was glance in her direction. She was quiet, reserved, didn't seem to talk to many people. Her friend approached her once while the band was playing, urging her to go on the dance floor, and that's when he first noticed that she signed to her friend. Growing up with a hard-of-hearing dad, he could understand the brunette, and he almost laughed out loud when she told her friend that she'd talked to three other girls who were there for Trek.

His name was actually Trek. Whether that was completely made up or some nickname, Pete didn't know. Trek brought women to the bar all the time, but not for screwing. He wanted this bar wall to wall with as many women as possible because where the women were, the men would follow and the band took a small cut of the drinks on the nights they played.

"Switch sides?" Pete asked Dimitri, who shrugged. He wasn't much of a conversationalist, and if it wasn't for the cute brunette he desperately wanted to talk to, Pete would have been bored most of the night working beside Dimitri.

Pete went right over to the brunette, wiping down the bar top and taking the empties piled along the bar. "Another?"

She shook her head and glanced toward the dance floor where her friend was now dancing with Trek while the band took a break. They were surrounded by a lot of other girls who looked as if they might start a brawl.

"You sure?" he asked her.

Her cheeks reddened, and she shook her head once more, not speaking. He knew how reserved his dad was about using his voice, so he didn't want to push her, but at the same time, he wanted to have a conversation with her.

After helping a few more customers, he noticed she kept staring at her phone then out at the dance floor. Fuck it. He went to her end of the bar. He could tell she was about to slide off the stool, probably tell her friend that she was leaving, and he knew he might never see her again. Something inside him said he couldn't let that happen.

She was already smiling and shaking her head as he approached, but he lifted his hands and signed, Water? A shot of tequila? What do I have to get you to stay a little longer?

Her head rocked back and a giggle he could barely hear over the music came out of her. She situated herself on the stool and signed back, A shot of tequila, I guess.

My name is Pete, *he signed.*

Bea.

And for the rest of the night, Pete was the worst bartender to everyone except Bea.

I crack my neck and flex my fingers. God, it feels so good to have a story that can't stop coming to me. It's as if it's just flowing out of me, and I can barely type fast enough to keep up.

Grabbing a yogurt that I brought with me this morning, I sit in the stillness of the cottage, smiling to myself. Hudson is picking up Adley from preschool today. I have the entire cottage to myself for a day of uninterrupted writing, and for the first time in a long time, I'm excited by the prospect.

I walk over to the couch, ready to write another chapter, when I spot a white shuttle pull up in the driveway. I figure they must have the wrong house, but then I see the script on the side and sigh. Northern Lights Retirement Sint Center.

There goes my productive day of writing. I turn my cochlear implants back on.

Alice and Jean get out of the van with bags of stuff in hand, two men trailing behind. Glancing around, I wonder if I can sneak out somewhere, but they all stare at my SUV in the driveway, and I hear them arguing about who they think it is, making my escape impossible.

I'm thrown when they don't knock on the door but use a key to gain entry. Since Adley is with Hudson, I can go home and write, although I feel as if there's some kind of magic here helping me get the words in. Still, I pack up my stuff.

"Palmer?" Alice stops in the doorway with some other friends of my great-grandma.

They've tried to fill the shoes of my great-grandma Dori and her friend Ethel Greene, two meddling grandmas who pushed all their kids toward the loves of their lives. No one can fill their shoes though.

I wave, reaching for my coat.

"We didn't know that Lance had given the key out. So, you're the next, huh?" Alice says.

I nod.

"Why doesn't she speak?" a man behind Alice asks. I've never seen him before, and I'm not sure if he's the new driver or what.

"She's deaf," Jean says.

Well then.

"It's hard of hearing," Alice corrects. "Sorry, Palmer, this is a new resident, Neil. He's our driver now."

I wave and smile.

"Why did they give you the key?" Alice asks, nosy as always.

"Um..." I say, and Neil smiles as if I'm a toddler in the middle of a tantrum and using my words. None of them sign, so I have no choice but to speak unless I want to grab a piece of paper and write it all out, which I don't. "I'm having a hard time writing."

Neil's smile grows bigger, and I become more irritated.

"Oh…so no problems with Hudson?" Jean asks.

This type of thing is one reason I almost didn't move home after finding out I was pregnant with Adley, but I knew that even with Hudson's help, I would need the help of my family as well. And truth be told, although they're big and loud and nosy as all get out, I love them. I loved growing up in Lake Starlight, and I wanted that for Adley too. But everyone in town knowing everything can be a bit much sometimes. Especially with Buzz Wheel, an app that reports on the secrets of its town residents.

"Who's Hudson?" Neil asks.

Jean stares blankly as though she's already had it with him. "Her daughter's dad."

"Her husband?" Neil asks.

I slide on my coat, and Alice approaches, shaking her head. "No. No. We'll leave. We just wanted to get out of the home for a while. They were trying to get us to do a Richard Simmons workout video. Where do you think they dug that thing up from?"

"It's okay, I can head home."

"I'm lost. She has a husband and a daughter, and she comes here? Sounds like trouble." Neil chimes in with his two cents.

"They aren't married," Jean informs him.

"Who isn't married?" Neil asks, talking louder each time he opens his mouth.

"Palmer and Hudson. They aren't married." Jean shakes her head and gives me an apologetic look.

"But they have a daughter?"

"Oh, you old fool, you don't have to be married to have a child." Jean crosses her arms and turns away from him.

"So, they're divorced?" Neil continues trying to understand my life.

"No," Alice and Jean say in unison.

"What happened to being an honorable gentleman and marrying the woman you get in trouble?"

"Oh jeez." Jean sighs. "Hudson didn't get Palmer in trouble. They slept together and conceived a baby as friends. Now, they raise that daughter and live side-by-side. It's really a great situation for Adley."

"Who's Adley?" Neil asks.

"Don't answer," Alice tells Jean and turns to me. "I am glad I ran into you, though, because we picked your book for book club. Everyone at Northern Lights is going to read it."

"Um…I'm sorry?" I had to hear her wrong. Why would they pick my book?

"We picked one of your books. We can't wait! We're just waiting for all of the paperbacks to arrive, then we're going to read in chapters and have discussions. Would you be willing to come and talk?"

This has to be a joke. A group of senior citizens wants to read my romance novel? I mean, I know a lot of my readers are older, but I don't know them personally. Just the mental image of Alice and Jean reading my sex scenes makes me want to cringe. People always think it comes from personal experience. It's fiction, people.

"Please. We've never had an author at our meetings before," Alice says.

Jean clears her throat.

"Well, we had that one who wrote a book on the habits of bird mating, but that isn't the same thing as a fiction writer." Alice widens her eyes at me, and I see the resemblance to her granddaughter, Aubrey, who is Calista's best friend.

I would have never wanted anyone to tell my great-grandma Dori no, so I find myself nodding. "Okay."

She opens her arms and pulls me into her, although her head reaches my breasts, and I'm afraid I'm going to smother her. Drawing back, she keeps her hands on my arms. "Thank you. I can't wait to tell everyone. I'll be in touch on dates and times. We should leave you to it then. If we enjoy this book, maybe you'll become a regular, and we'll read all your books." She looks over at the table.

Then she walks over and grabs the white envelope there, seeing my name on it. Calista told me that Alice was the one who first gave her the key to the cabin, that Great-Grandma Dori put her and Jean in charge of getting it to Calista.

"Have you read it?"

I shake my head. "Not ready." Maybe the truth will stop Alice from continuing to pry into my life.

She nods. "Well, you should soon. There's a reason your cousin picked this moment to give you the key. Whatever is in that letter will help guide you along this journey."

My eyebrows scrunch. I don't understand what she's talking about.

She sets the letter back down and takes my hands. "Just read it, please...soon. I'm saying this as a grandma. It's important, right, Gilbert?" She turns to the old man who has remained silent this whole time.

"She was quite adamant when she left them with me." Gilbert, who used to be the town lawyer, must have been in charge of Great-Grandma Dori's things, but I know Calista has all the letters now.

I nod, though I'll open it when I feel like it, without anyone forcing me to.

"Well, let's go, gang." And just like that, Alice is back to business.

"We're going back?" Neil says. "I thought we were staying here?"

"Get a clue," Jean says and walks out with Gilbert following her.

They leave, and I shut the door, grabbing my laptop again.

I write until late, and although I could spend the night, I want my own bed, so I drive home. The lights are on at Hudson's. When I look at the time, I know he's likely giving Adley a bath right now. Boy, do I miss her already, and it was just this morning when I saw her last. I could easily go over there, Hudson wouldn't care, but with Theresa in his life, I feel as though we're going to have to start maintaining some boundaries. Boundaries we've never had before.

I park in my one car detached garage, and as I walk to my door, I hear Hudson whisper-shout my name. Turning around, I walk toward his back door. He's standing there barefoot in jeans and a sweatshirt, his hair messy. It's my favorite look on him.

"What's up?" I ask.

"We have a problem."

nine

HUDSON

"Where have you been anyway?" I ask Palmer.

I don't mention that I've been watching her driveway all night, wondering when she would get back, imagining her in Matt's hotel room or something. It's none of my business, I know.

"I was...out." She steps into my house and into my kitchen. "Is she still up?"

"No, she crashed early. Took her to the slopes after preschool."

"Again, huh?"

I sheepishly grin because I'd live on the slopes if I could, and she's worried Adley will follow in my footsteps and not discover anything else that interests her. Palmer just doesn't get it because she hasn't done it.

"She asked," I clarify.

"Uh-huh, and no pushing from you, I suspect." She grins.

I chuckle and throw my fingers through my hair.

"It's getting pretty long," she says, touching my thick hair.

A bolt of electricity shoots through my body when her fingernails graze my scalp. I jump back, and she startles.

"What?"

I shake my head. "I just got a shock," I say, unsure how to explain what happened.

Palmer has always touched my hair—hell, one time she even cut it. I had to wear a hat for a month afterward, but we still laugh at why we thought it was a good idea at the time.

"So, what's the problem?" She drops her bag on the kitchen chair.

For whatever reason, that act makes me realize how comfortable we both are at each other's houses. What will happen if Theresa and I get more serious? This comfort level we have with each other will all fade away, and it will affect Adley, I know it.

"Come over to the fridge." I walk her to the picture Adley drew at preschool today that she proudly showed me when I picked her up. All her artwork is on my fridge, so I had to put this one up, but I'm not sure what some people will think when they see it. "Adley drew a picture today."

"Oh nice. Can you even decipher what it is?" She laughs and looks at me. "Remember last time when we thought it was a mouse pooping, but it was the Easter Bunny dropping eggs?"

"Yeah, this is a bit different." I point at it, and Palmer gets closer, her fingers on the edge of the paper.

"Oh." Her mouth twists into a frown.

"Yeah, oh."

On one side of the picture is Palmer and me with Adley between us, holding each of our hands, and there's another woman on the other side, far away. She's wearing a dress, and her hair is blonde. She has a straight line for her mouth while Palmer, Adley, and I are all smiling.

"Does Adley not like Theresa? I thought she did?" I'm hoping Palmer can fill in some blanks because I was thrown when I saw it.

"Me too. She lets Theresa do her hair, and she's never said a bad word about her." Palmer does appear surprised.

"Have you ever said anything about Theresa that maybe she could've overheard?"

Palmer tilts her head and narrows her eyes. "Seriously?"

"I'm just trying to figure this out."

"So, you're going to blame me?"

I open the fridge and grab a beer. "I know what you think of her," I say without thinking it through. Big mistake.

"And what is that?" The thing with Palmer is that she doesn't back down. Now that I started this conversation, she's going to see it all the way through even if I say I didn't mean it.

"I just mean that you guys are very different." I turn away from her because, in truth, she's kind of scary when she's like this.

"I'm aware, but do you think I would talk badly about her in front of Adley? Give me a little credit."

I prop myself up on the counter, taking a pull from my beer. "I didn't mean intentionally. I meant that maybe you said something to your mom or Harper, and she overheard you. I get it, Theresa can be a little—"

She signs a million miles a minute, which happens a lot when she's mad. *I'm not even going there. She's fine. You like her. I've dealt with her for the past few months. If you want her to be a part of your life, then I would only encourage Adley to like her, too.*

"Okay…I'm sorry."

You should be. I can't believe you think I would do that. She points at the picture. *I have no idea where this is coming from, but did you try asking her?*

"No."

Why not?

Because I was afraid of what Adley would say. If she doesn't like Theresa, it's going to blow up. We're going to have problems to deal with, and I hate dealing with problems and other people's emotions.

Before I can even respond, she's signing again. *You're scared because if she says she doesn't like her, then you have to examine how strongly you feel about Theresa and whether she's worth fighting for.*

Damn Palmer, I hate it when she's right, and she always fucking is. The woman has been able to read me like a book since the day we met. Her smug smile says she knows it too.

Listen, Hudson, I get you never thought you'd settle down with someone, but you seem to like her. You've kept her around longer than anyone else.

Except for you, I think, but that's different. We share a daughter.

"We're just dating," I fire back.

It's been a long night, and I'm going home and getting some sleep. I suggest tomorrow morning you have a conversation with your daughter about that. She points at the fridge. *Night, night.*

She grabs her stuff and walks out the back door. I could follow her, continue this conversation, ask her about Theresa and tell her my worries. But what if it comes out about how I don't like seeing her and Matt together and then things get weird between us? I don't even understand it myself. We should both just get some sleep and figure out these problems tomorrow.

MORNING COMES TOO FAST, and when I finally get Adley ready and at the table, all I can do is stare at the drawing. Palmer is so much better at this than me. This is her realm as a parent, not mine. But I need to man up and ask my three-year-old. Damn, I'm pathetic.

"Hey, Ad?" I ask, pouring a coffee with my back to her.

"Yeah," she says, and I hear her spoon some cereal from her bowl.

"You know this drawing you did yesterday at school?" I turn and face her, leaning back against the counter.

"Yeah." Her attention is only on her cereal, scooping out the marshmallows.

"You know you have to eat the entire bowl, not just the marshmallows."

She doesn't answer me, continuing to move her spoon around the bowl, scooping up the floating marshmallows.

I sit at the table with her, and my eye catches on the drawing again. "Adley?"

"Uh-huh," she says with a full mouth.

"The drawing yesterday."

She glances up and looks back down. "Uh-huh."

Just bite the bullet, Hudson. You're the dad here, the authority. Stop thinking about your own hang-ups.

"Is that Theresa with the blonde hair?" I ask.

"I gave her a pretty dress." She spoons the last marshmallow and reaches for the box.

I snag it and point at the bowl, and her shoulders deflate. "Why is she upset?"

She glances over her shoulder and looks at the picture as if she doesn't remember drawing it in the first place. "Because you're with Mommy," she says matter-of-factly.

"Why would that upset her?"

She finally looks up from her cereal with a serious face. "She looks like that every time we're with Mommy."

My stomach pitches, and I open my mouth, only to close it again.

She goes back to her cereal, scooping up the cereal and milk that's still full of sugar. But at least it's a little more nutritious than just the marshmallows.

"No, she doesn't," I finally respond.

She nods. "Yes, she does."

I retrace my memory to all the times they've had to interact, and yes, it's awkward, but Theresa just seems uncomfortable, not mad. "I've never noticed that."

She nods and finishes off her cereal. "Can I watch TV until we leave?"

I start to nod but stop. "Wait. Do you like Theresa?" There. The question is out there.

She stares at me so long that I'm not sure what she's going to say. "Yeah, but I like Mommy more."

"Well, of course."

Then she frowns. "She's not going to be my new mommy, right?"

I blink and blink again. "No." I shake my head. "Mommy will always be your mommy, nothing changes that."

She sits back in her chair. "Why don't you and Mommy sleep together?"

My heart rate spikes, and my breath comes out unsteady. Why is she asking this? I look behind me, hoping Palmer might surprise us this morning, but her car is already gone. I'm trying to convince myself she's not having breakfast with Matt.

Palmer is a creature of habit, and she loves her house. There have been weeks where she's been writing, and I'm not sure she's left, having food delivered to her. She came home late last night and now is gone early this morning. I don't understand why the change in her behavior.

"Daddy," Adley says. "Holden said he went into his mommy and daddy's bedroom because he had a nightmare, and they sleep in the same bed."

"Yeah, some mommies and daddies do."

"I told him my mommy and daddy don't sleep in the same house. He laughed at me."

My shoulders sag. Fuck a duck, there is no way we're here already.

"Marcy asked if you were divorced. What's divorced?"

I look out the window to make sure Palmer hasn't returned. Where is she when I need her? "We're not divorced. You have to be married to be divorced."

"Huh?" She tilts her cute little face to the side.

"Some mommies and daddies get married and then…"

Her innocent blue eyes stare up at me as though I hold all the knowledge in the world, and it's scary as shit. "Then what?"

"Well, they don't want to be married anymore."

Her forehead scrunches. "Why?"

"A lot of reasons. Sometimes they just fall out of love. Other times, one person isn't happy."

"Is that why you and Mommy aren't married?"

Jeez, her gaze is so intense. How am I intimidated by a three-year-old?

"No, I love your mommy."

"Then get married!"

I glance at the kitchen clock, wishing I had the excuse that we had to hurry and pack up and leave.

"It's a kind of different love," I say.

"Like how you love me?" she smiles.

I shake my head and ruffle her hair that I should really brush. "No, I have the most love for you. I love you more than anyone else in the world."

"You can't marry me." She giggles.

Jesus, this conversation has taken a turn.

"Of course I can't marry you. Smart girl." Hopefully she doesn't tell her teacher that her daddy wants to marry her. Wanting this conversation over with, I stand and dump out my coffee in the sink, rinsing it down. "We should do your hair."

I rush out of the kitchen and into the bathroom to get the brush and ponytail holders. Once I'm alone, I inhale and exhale a deep breath, happy that the conversation is over—for now at least, because I never really explained it all. I just need to keep her busy until preschool, then I'll call Palmer, and we can figure out how to handle this new stage. I thought the worst part of parenting was when she woke up at all hours of the night, but no one told me it would get harder as she got older. What the hell?

PALMER

I leave early for the cabin, and because it's a little warmer today, some fog has settled in, and it's harder to find, but I manage. When I get in, I slip off my boots, take off my jacket, and sit on the couch before pulling out my laptop, ready to get as many words in as I can.

The email from my editor is sitting unanswered until I see how much I can get done today. My mom is going to pick up Adley from school even though it's Hudson's day because he has to work.

I sit on the couch, the same side I've sat on every day since the words started flowing and open my manuscript. And just like every other time, the words are on the tips of my fingers, waiting for me to type them.

Bea was shaken. The hot bartender understood sign language. The bar had been way too loud for her talk, not that she enjoyed using her voice much anyway, so it was perfect.

And then, people were leaving and the bar had become emptier. Nia came up and asked if Bea wanted Trek to drive her home, but Bea politely shook her head. She'd figure something out—get an Uber or something. But she wasn't going to sit in the back seat while Nia and Trek wanted to be alone.

Nia glanced at the bartender and turned so only Bea could see her lips. "He's a cutie. Go home with him."

Although he had been giving Bea a lot of attention and a few free drinks, she thought he was just being nice because she was sitting alone in a bar filled with groups. This wasn't a townie bar where people just came in by themselves for a drink. It was a club where people, especially women, came in groups.

Bea pulled Nia down so she could say into her ear, "That's not how it works. Go have fun with the drummer."

"Hopefully he knows how to use his stick." She laughed and kissed Bea on the cheek.

Bea's eyes followed Nia as she hooked her arm through Trek's, and they left the bar.

The bartender, Pete, came over and wiped down the spot where two guys had spilled a beer. "She's going to regret that decision."

Bea shrugged. Nia rarely regretted anything. She had the motto that you only lived life once, so you might as well do what you want, when you want. Bea admired Nia to a certain extent. Although when Bea had left her small hometown in Idaho, all she'd wanted to do was travel and see the world. She wasn't as carefree as Nia.

She lifted her hands and signed, She won't. He might.

Pete laughed, and his eyes sparkled. She was really starting to like this guy. He leaned over the bar, arms crossed and resting on the bar top, and all she could do was focus on his lips. Which was a great excuse to stare at them since she was always reading lips.

"I'm off in five, let me give you a ride."

What did she really know about this guy? Her mom would

kill her if she found out Bea had gotten in the car with some stranger. All those crime stories Bea watched on TV played out in her head as she debated what to do.

Pete reached into his back pocket and placed his license in front of her on the bar. Take a picture, send it to whoever you want. Tell them I'm driving you home. If you go missing, they'll be able to track me down.

How do I know this is even you? *Bea raised her eyebrows.*

You don't, but...*he dropped his wallet in front of her.* Go ahead.

Bea shook her head. She wasn't one to pry into someone else's life. Pete had been nice to her all night which she took as pity, but maybe he was interested in her.

Look through it. *He pushed his wallet closer to her.*

The brown leather was worn along the edges, and Bea opened the fold, unsure if she should or not, but she knew it would put her mind at ease.

Inside were two credit cards with the same name as the license. There was a voter's registration card, which made her laugh. When Pete leaned in to see, she pulled it out. He just didn't seem the type to keep up with politics. She didn't bother to look at the cash he had—that would be another level of nosy. Satisfied, she shut the wallet and slid it over to him.

That's it? I offer you my entire life, and you barely look?

Bea contemplated her reply carefully, not wanting to be too forward, but she really liked him and wanted something to happen between them. I'd rather get to know you by talking with you some more rather than finding out that way.

He smiled, and even though she was sitting, her knees felt weak. A ride home then?

She looked up through her dark eyelashes, bit her lip, and nodded.

He went over to the other bartender and told him something, then grabbed his coat from a cubby behind the bar. Bea thought her heart was going to beat out of her chest as Pete walked the length of space behind the bar toward her, his smile permanently in place as if he felt lucky that she'd accepted his ride home.

He lifted the bar top and walked through the opening. She slid off her stool and realized how short she was compared to him once he was closer.

"Ready?" he said, and she nodded. He held his hand out, and she walked in front of him toward the door.

Once outside, the cold air whipped around them. The only light came from the light poles in the parking lot. Darkness surrounded them in the small mountain town. He led her over to an SUV that had seen better days. It was rusty along the edges, and there were stickers on the back about snowboarding and different brands that made snowboarding equipment. He had a rack on top she guessed usually held his boards.

He opened the door, and she slid inside, surprised at how clean it was. She'd half expected to find empty energy drink cans and fast-food bags everywhere, but other than salt damage on the floor mats, it was spotless. It even smelled nice, as if he knew this would happen and had just come from the car wash.

He rounded the SUV and climbed in, then started the car, pointing the heating vents in her direction. "I don't want to take you home."

Oh shit, you are going to kill me. Let me call my mom first.

He chuckled, and those eyes sparkled again. "I meant more along the lines of do you want to get something to eat?"

She felt her cheeks warm. He was just as interested as her and that brought on the flutters in her stomach. Sure.

He nodded, and before she realized it, they were pulling away from the bar. She had a really good feeling about this guy and hoped her gut was leading her in the right direction. But when she peeked at his profile, she didn't care much even if it was the wrong one. She wanted something to happen tonight, and she'd take it for herself if she had to.

BY THE TIME I get home, it's past dinner. My stomach growls as I pull into the driveway and into my garage. I have nothing much to eat at my place because I'm planning on going shopping before I pick up Adley tomorrow. Although I'm half tempted to ask my mom to pick her up again. This story is consuming me in the best way, and I need to finish it.

Hudson's back door opens. "Hey."

I groan because if this has to do with Adley not liking Theresa, I don't feel like dealing with it. At least until after this book is done.

"What's wrong?" I ask.

"Where were you?"

I'm not sure when he started caring so much where I was. "Working."

"Are you going to Brewed Awakenings or something now?" He lifts his wrist as if to check the time on his watch.

"I'm just..." I've never kept a secret from him, and I debate telling him. But I like having this place to myself, and I don't want to ruin my mojo. "I'll tell you later."

"Were you with Matt?"

I blink, surprised by his question or why he thinks I'd keep that from him. "No. Why?"

He shakes his head. "Sorry. It's none of my business."

I don't say anything because he's right. I'm not asking him intimate details about him and Theresa.

"Your mom made spaghetti. Want some?"

My stomach clenches at the offer, making the decision for me. I walk over, thinking I'll just take some to go, but when I walk into his kitchen, I see that won't be the case. He has two plates out and a fresh batch of garlic bread on the table.

"Your mom left a loaf to make for you," he says, after seeing my quizzical look at what appears like a setup for a date.

"You didn't eat with Adley, how come? Are you trying to butter me up?"

He laughs. "No, why?"

I tilt my head. "What is all this, Hudson?"

"I do this all the time when you have a tight deadline." He scoops two big helpings of spaghetti onto the plates.

He definitely wants something.

"No, you keep Adley a little more over at your place and leave food on my counter for me to eat when I take a break. This"—I put my hand out—"is not what usually happens. The last time you did something like this was when you wanted to start Adley on the snowboard."

He bites his lip to keep him from smiling because he knows I'm right. The look is sexy as hell, and my libido goes into overdrive, which is weird. God, it's got to be because I've had such a long dry spell. I really should call Matt back.

I sign, *Is Theresa moving in?*

"God no. Why would you ask that?"

My head rocks back, surprised by his quick denial.

Maybe because she's your girlfriend, and I've noticed she's over here a lot.

"Yeah, I guess I get why you asked, but I'm not ready for that."

I decide to keep it to myself that I'm sure Theresa *is* ready for it. Sometimes Hudson lives in LaLa Land and is the last to realize what others around him already have. *Then what is this all about?*

We both sit at the table in front of our plates before he says, "Our daughter."

"What about her?" I pick up my fork because I'm about to eat my right arm.

"She wants to know why we don't sleep in the same bed and if we're divorced. I think we've come to the age where she realizes our situation is different, and she doesn't understand."

My stomach suddenly sours, even as hungry as I am, and I put my fork down and sit back in my chair. We all knew eventually it was coming, although in this day and age, there are so many family dynamics you could fool yourself into thinking that the old-school typical family isn't the norm anymore. But here we are.

"Did you explain it to her?"

He finishes chewing and buys himself some time by sipping his water.

"Hudson?"

"I tried. She's like a little Barbara Walters."

I laugh. It's true. Our daughter doesn't give up easily when she wants to figure out something. It isn't hard to figure out Hudson's ulterior motive now. "And this dinner is so I'll talk to her?"

"I just…"

"I'll make you a deal—we can talk to her together." I

nod toward the fridge, which is now missing the drawing of pissed-off Theresa. "The drawing spurred this?"

"It spurred me asking her. I was caught off guard."

I pick up my fork again and spin it. "Okay, I guess we have no choice but to go at this together. It's parenting, right? Just give me until tomorrow night."

"Why then?" he asks.

"Because I have plans."

He sits back and crosses his arms. "What kind of plans? You've been secretive lately."

"I have a book to finish. I've been writing."

"But not at home?"

"No, not at home." I bury my head in my plate.

Thankfully he lets the topic go, but I'm not sure how long I can hold him off. Adley got her perseverance from her father after all.

eleven

HUDSON

I should be concentrating on Theresa right now. She's talking about a problem student in her class, and my entire attention should be on her, but it's not. I can't stop wondering where Palmer has been going when she disappears. I was with Matt this morning for training, and he asked me about her, so I know she's not spending her entire day with him. It makes her disappearances more of a mystery, though. Could she be seeing someone else?

Could the writing be coming naturally at some other guy's place?

If so, I can't believe Buzz Wheel hasn't reported anything. A Bailey finding love is always a priority on that stupid app.

"Hudson!" Theresa waves her hand in front of my face. "Where are you? Because you sure aren't at this table."

"Sorry." I pick up my beer and take a sip. "Go on."

"No, it's just getting me all riled up anyway. Is something going on?" She picks up her fork and stabs some lettuce onto it. We went out for pizza, but she demanded we get a salad too, for nutrition's sake, but she's only eating salad, and I'm only eating pizza.

"Nothing's going on." I would never tell her I'm hung up on who Palmer is spending her time with unless I wanted us to have a fight.

"You're lying."

"I'm not."

She gives me a look that clearly says she doesn't believe me and continues to eat her salad. "How is Adley doing?"

"Good," I say, not wanting to broach that topic either.

"And Matt? Training?"

"Good."

She puts her fork down, lifts her napkin from her lap, and wipes her mouth. She replaces the napkin, leans back in her chair, folds her hands together in her lap, and stares at me. She's mad. "Is that the only word in your vocabulary tonight? It's Friday night, and finally, neither of us has our children, and instead of having an actual conversation when we've barely talked these last three days, you're answering everything with one-word answers."

She has a point. I wish I was into tonight, but I'm not. I'm not sure I can be honest about all of Adley's questions without causing a fight. Theresa is so sensitive these days, though it wasn't like that when we first started dating. Then again, she's divorced and surely her daughter has had questions of her own. Maybe she's the perfect person to talk to about this.

"Adley is questioning Palmer's and my relationship." There.

Theresa shrugs. "Well, it is unusual."

Fucking hell. I should have kept my mouth shut.

"Theresa." I sigh.

She raises her hand. "Sorry, okay, okay. She's in

preschool now, and other kids are sharing stories about their home lives. She's going to think she's different."

"Are you kidding me? Only a third of marriages work in this country now. There has to be parents who live separately in her class." I pick up another piece of pizza.

"Yeah, but they're divorced. You and Palmer were never married, and you get along like...well, I mean, you're friends."

"Which should be a good thing, no?"

She nods. "It is, but all Adley understands is it's different. Either parents are married and live together, or they're divorced and live apart."

"Palmer and I live apart."

Her head rocks back and forth. "Yes, but you stop by each other's houses all the time. I guarantee you're over there or she's at your house on days that aren't your days. There's probably been times you've eaten together when one of you didn't have to be there."

I shake my head in frustration. "I see all that as a good thing."

She chuckles. "You're confusing what's good for Adley and what is making her feel different from the other kids. I mean, when Riley is at my ex's, I talk to her once or if she needs to talk to me. Otherwise she's with him, and I see her when we exchange back."

My stomach twists at the thought of Palmer and me being like that. We've never had papers drawn up. We just talk to each other and make plans. "God, it sounds like..."

"That's divorce, Hudson. Most divorced people don't like each other."

I think she's wrong. I've met plenty of divorced people who can be civil for the kid's sake. "I don't plan on changing anything with our arrangement."

She sighs and picks up her fork as if it bothers her. "I'm well aware."

Silence. Neither of us say anything until we finish our meal, and the waiter asks us if we want a box for the pizza. I pay the bill, pick up the box of pizza, and lead Theresa back to my truck.

"Whose house are we going to stay at tonight?" she asks.

I hate the fact that I want to drop her off at her house and go home alone. It's not her fault my head is a mess right now. Excuses fill my brain, but she'll see through each one. We haven't had any alone time lately and haven't had sex in weeks.

"Mine?" I ask because then I can find out if Palmer asked her mom to watch Adley again. Shit. That's none of my business. I shake my head. "Never mind, let's go to yours."

A wide smile forms on her face. "Great."

"If you wanted to go to your place, why did you give me a choice?"

She shrugs, putting on her seat belt. "You always want to be at your house, and this way I have you all to myself." She leans over the center console and puckers her lips.

I bend forward, give her a chaste kiss, then face forward and start the truck.

She grabs my hand. This is what I need. A night with Theresa will clear my head, take it off whatever Palmer is doing and back to where it should be. We drive through the streets of Lake Starlight to the downtown residential area and pull up at Theresa's small white house with black shutters. I park in her small driveway and remove my seat belt. I'm about to turn off the ignition when my phone rings over the Bluetooth in my car.

Palmer's name flashes on the screen.

Theresa stares at me, but I press accept. "Hey, what's up?"

"Hudson." Her voice is panicked, and it's clear she's upset. "It's Adley. She was at that indoor park place with my mom, and she fell off the platform."

"Is she okay?" I put the truck in reverse and strap my seat belt back on as I'm moving backward.

"She's at the hospital. I'm driving there right now. Thank God my aunt Stella's best friend, Allie, is working."

"Are you sure you can drive? I'll come get you," I say, hearing her crying. I do not need her to get into an accident.

She's quiet for a moment, then a deep voice speaks. "I'm driving. She's good. We'll meet you there."

Matt.

So, she was with Matt. She had her mom watch Adley so she could go on a date.

"Good. We'll see you in a few minutes," Theresa says and clicks the end call button because I'm stunned.

I'm not sure if that's the first time Theresa's ever heard Palmer speak, but if it is, she doesn't remark on it. I'm surprised Palmer was speaking in front of Matt. Either she's comfortable enough with him that she hasn't been using sign language all night, or she was so panicked she didn't think to text me rather than calling.

I drive to the hospital on autopilot and fly into a parking spot, turning off the ignition and rushing toward the emergency room entrance.

Theresa walks fast beside me, trying to keep up with my strides.

We run into Palmer and Matt at the nurses' station. She's already informing them who we are.

The nurse looks up at us. "All four of you can't go back. I'll allow two." She puts up her fingers.

There's no question, it's Palmer and me. She buzzes us in and tells us which room to go to.

"I don't understand, why was she with your mom?" I ask as soon as we're on the other side of the doors.

Palmer glances at me. "Excuse me?"

"I'm just saying, this was your night. She should've been with you, not your mom."

She stops in the hallway for a moment and tugs on my jacket sleeve. "What the fuck, Hudson? You're giving me shit about going on a date?"

"I'm not giving you shit about going on a date. It's that we're here when she should've been with you. Schedule your dates on your days off parenting Adley."

She makes this sound as though I'm unbelievable and stomps forward.

"I'm just saying." I walk beside her.

Her head whips in my direction. "You know how many times over the years I've taken your nights so you could go out?"

"If you wanted to go out with Matt, why didn't you ask me?"

She shakes her head. "This was an accident, Hudson. That's all. It has nothing to do with who was watching her. So what if I wanted to go out, and my parents wanted some time with their granddaughter?"

I shake my head. "Your parents always want to take her somewhere fun."

"Sue them. They're her grandparents!"

We reach the room, and Palmer walks through the door before me. Her mom stands from the chair next to the bed

Adley's little body is tucked into. Her dad stops pacing to look at us.

"Mommy! Daddy! Cherry!" Adley is all smiles and holds up a popsicle as her red lips grin. The first thing I notice are the stitches along her forehead and the side of her head.

"Hey, kiddo, how are you?" I walk to the side of the bed and kiss the part of her forehead that isn't injured.

"What happened?" Palmer grabs Adley's hand and looks at her mom.

"She was playing with some other kids at that indoor park at the mall. One kid went down the fire pole, and she followed. I was screaming for her not to, but I couldn't get to her in time." Sedona, Palmer's mom, starts to cry, and Palmer's dad, Jamison, puts his arm around his wife.

"It was just an accident," he says.

"Gran'ma!" Adley says. "Don't cry."

"Mom, Dad's right, it was just an accident." Palmer stares at me when she says it.

"Yeah, Sedona. Coulda happened to anyone," Jamison says.

Allie Greene walks into the room and puts on hand sanitizer. She's Palmer's aunt's best friend and works as a nurse here at the hospital. "Oh good, you guys are here. The doctor was looking at the scans, and he'll be in shortly." She stands at the end of the bed. "I'm glad I was here."

"I'm so happy you are too." Palmer smiles.

"As long as the scans are clear, Adley here is good to go."

Just then a doctor walks into the room, and Palmer's eyebrows raise because the guy is good-looking and young.

"Hello, I'm Dr. Michaels."

Palmer smiles and waves.

"I assume you're the parents?"

Palmer nods.

"Yes," I say.

"Well, Adley's scans came back, and it all looks good. She did have to get a number of stitches, which will need to be taken out in a week or two depending on how she's healing. And Allie is going to give you some information on things to look out for over the next couple of days. If you notice any of them, bring her right back."

Palmer nods. Even Sedona can't stop staring at this guy.

"Thanks," I say with a nod.

"Any questions?" he asks, looking around the group of us.

"No," I say, annoyed by both Palmer and her mom's reaction to this guy.

"Okay then. Allie will get Adley's discharge papers. Good to meet you guys." He walks out.

"Wow," Palmer says.

Allie laughs. "Yeah, he tends to get that kind of reaction. He's new here. Fisher hates when I work with him." She rolls her eyes and chuckles.

"Let's get her home," I say, wanting to be done with this hot doctor business.

"Let me get her discharge papers and the info the doctor mentioned, and I'll be right back."

"We'll give you some privacy," Sedona says, still with tears in her eyes.

Adley's grandparents kiss her goodbye and leave the room. Palmer and I hold Adley's hands, thankful it's nothing more than some stitches.

"That must have been quite a fall," I say, eyeing Adley's stitches.

Palmer stares across the bed at me with a pissed-off expression. "And you see how guilty my mom already feels, so I don't want to hear it."

Guilt racks me. How many times has something almost happened to Adley on my watch? I'm letting my feelings about Palmer and Matt get mixed up with the fact that Adley had an accident, and that's not fair to Palmer or her mom.

"I'm sorry. I was just scared and worried about Adley." And not at all pissed off that Palmer was on a date with Matt. What is wrong with me? "Honestly, Palm, I'm sorry. I should have never said anything."

Her shoulders sink, and she nods. "Okay."

I grab her hand. A tear trickles down her cheek, and I round the bed, pulling her into my body, acutely aware that Adley is watching us closely. Palmer wraps her arms around my torso, and her back shakes as she sobs. I run my hands down her back. The smell of her shampoo floats up to my nose, taking me back to the night we conceived Adley.

What the hell?

But I keep holding her, not wanting to let her go.

"Hey!" I turn to see Theresa walk through the door. She stops in her tracks when she sees Palmer in my arms. "Oh."

Well, shit.

twelve

A throat clears from behind me, and Hudson pulls away from me with a force I'm not prepared for, sending my hip into the railing of Adley's hospital bed.

Ouch.

"Theresa, hey," he says, sounding nervous.

The look on Theresa's face says she's misunderstood what was just happening. "When Sedona and Jamison came out, I figured it would be okay to come in. I wanted to check on Adley."

I hate that she talks as if she's friends with my parents. She'd met them once, and it was in passing.

"Of course." Hudson puts his arm around her waist, leading her over to the hospital bed. "Her scans came back good, so they're getting her discharge papers together. It's just the stitches along her forehead that are coming with her."

"So not life-threatening. The way you two were clinging together..." Her eyes meet mine.

Usually I let her passive-aggressive comments go

because I'm not one to start shit, but I raise my hands to sign. Then I figure fuck it, she needs to hear this from me, in my own voice. "We didn't know the situation until we got in here. You know what it's like to fear that your child is injured. The relief made me emotional."

Her expression shifts so fast, I want to roll my eyes. Up until today, I've never had a problem with Theresa. Other than I have never thought she was a good fit for Hudson. She's so put together, I worry that one day she'll have Hudson at some office job, picking up Adley in a suit and tie, and I know he'd grow to resent it. I'd hate to see him turn into one of those guys who says yes to everything his wife wants because he's afraid of her wrath.

"Of course, I understand. I just always find your relationship so odd, it takes me back a bit. My ex wouldn't touch me unless he had to resuscitate me. And even then, it'd be questionable." She laughs, but no one else does.

Well, Hudson smiles to appease the situation. Jeez, it's already starting.

Thankfully, Theresa turns to Adley. "Sweetie, your grandma said you just jumped for the fire pole. Why would you jump?"

I eye Hudson with a not-so-nice expression. I'm annoyed she's in here, let alone judging my three-year-old's decisions.

"It looked fun." Adley smiles at her.

"But those other kids were older, right?"

I keep my gaze on Hudson because if he doesn't get Theresa out of here, I'm going to say something. It's not her job to scold my child. Even Adley's eyes are scrunched up.

"We don't need to talk about it now," Hudson says.

Adley turns to me. "Mommy?"

"Yeah." I take her hand.

"Can we go home?"

I lift my hands to sign, *As soon as Nurse Allie comes back with the paperwork.*

"Can I have another popsicle?" Her eyes are wide with excitement.

"We'll see," I say out loud. I take the popsicle stick out of her hand, throw it away, then turn toward Hudson. "If you two want to go, I'll get her home." Really what I mean is that if Theresa would like to leave, I'm happy to open the door for her.

"I'm not going anywhere," Hudson says. "I'll take her home."

"No, I can take her home." If he thinks I'm going to let my little girl out of my sight, he's mistaken.

"I'm not having Matt drive her home. If you want to be with her, you can come with me."

Hudson is an easygoing guy. Rarely does he get up in arms about anything. Except if it has to do with our daughter—like now, for instance. Our past tells me he won't let this go, so I give in to try to prevent an argument. We're already too tense with each other tonight.

"We took an Uber, so you can drive us both."

His eyes bore into mine for a few seconds. "Fine. We'll caravan it back to our houses."

"But we were going to go to..." Theresa says, and Hudson shoots her a glare. "Never mind."

Allie comes in with the discharge papers a minute later, thank goodness. We go over everything, and Theresa finally excuses herself when it's time to get Adley dressed.

I'm busy helping Adley put her arms in her shirt when Hudson says, "She doesn't know how to act in front of you. You make her nervous."

I glance at Adley who is now looking between us wide-eyed and raise my hands to sign while I speak. *Sweetie, Mommy and Daddy are going to talk in the hall for a quick second. Can you go sit in that chair and wait for us like a good girl?*

She shrugs. "Okay."

I nod toward the open door for Hudson to follow me. He does, and when we're outside, I close the door to the room, leaving it open just a sliver so I can hear if anything is awry inside the room. Then I turn to face Hudson with my arms crossed. "Why would I make Theresa nervous? I've never done anything to her."

"I don't know."

I shrug. "Then it's not my problem, it's hers."

"Jesus, Palmer, you could have some empathy and understanding. It's not like you've ever been warm and welcoming to her."

I stare at him for a beat before I answer. "I don't have to be welcoming. I'm not the one dating her."

"Exactly, she's *my* girlfriend, and she spends a lot of time with our daughter. Maybe Adley drew that picture because you're not so nice to Theresa," he whispers, as if our daughter might hear him through the door.

"Do not do that! Do not blame me for her inability to be in a room with me because she's insecure."

He shakes his head. "You're intimidating."

"No, I'm not, Hudson. You didn't think so when we first met."

He shakes his head with a smirk. "Yes, I did. How would you know what was in my head that night?"

"You approached me," I say.

"Because I was the bartender. It was my job. But you're different with Theresa. Standoffish. Cold at times."

I take a step closer to him. "I cannot believe you're

picking right now to have this conversation with me. What? Were you going to pop the question tonight or something?" I ignore the drop in my stomach just imagining the scene.

"Hell no, you know I'm not the settling down type, but she is a part of my life, and I'd like the two of you to get along. That's all I'm saying."

"Fine. I'll be nicer. Let's go." I turn around to go through the door, but my hand pauses on the handle because Theresa is at the far end of the hallway, which pisses me off because she was probably eavesdropping on our conversation. Great.

I leave Theresa for Hudson to deal with and go back into the room.

I pick up Adley off the chair and get her coat on then leave the room, passing Hudson and Theresa. When we enter the waiting room my parents get up from their chairs. Adley runs over to them as if she wasn't just in the room with them. My mom grabs her, lifting her off the floor, and hugs her tightly.

"You're going to cut off her breathing," I say jokingly.

"I'm so sorry. Grandma will make it up to you. We're going to Sweet Suga Things tomorrow, and I'm bringing you donuts tomorrow morning."

"Birthday cake ones?" Adley beams because it's her favorite flavor.

"Whatever you want, wee one," my dad says before kissing her cheek.

"Okay, you two. We're taking her home," I say, wanting to get out of here.

Matt returns from outside, pocketing his cell phone. "I heard it was just some stitches." He looks at Adley and back at me. "I've broken so many bones and hurt myself so much, stitches are like a paper cut now."

"You're not three," Hudson says. Thankfully, Matt doesn't seem to pick up on the note of ire in his voice.

"True. I'm glad she's good." He looks at me, and I give him a small smile.

I'm not sure I'm feeling anything with Matt. He's hot and all, and I wouldn't mind sleeping with him, but my life doesn't have room for anyone right now. Priority one is Adley, and priority two is getting this book finished.

We say goodbye to my parents and all head to Hudson's truck. I secure Adley in the car seat, then I sit on one side of her in the back and Matt sits on the other side. Theresa is up front with Hudson, and I watch her reach for his hand during the drive.

It shouldn't bother me. I've seen them be affectionate before. I've seen them kiss, so why does them holding hands feel like a gut punch? Adley grabs my hand as if she feels the same pain I do, but in reality, I'm sure she's sleepy. And probably wondering why Hudson and I were arguing since we don't normally do that in front of her.

I glance at Adley, and she has a small smile on her face, but her eyes are drooping. Oh, my sweet baby girl.

We pull into Hudson's driveway, and I remove Adley from the car seat and hold her.

"Hey, Palm?" Matt says.

It's weird to hear him use a shortened version of my name. Rarely does anyone do that except for Hudson every now and then. I turn to Matt before walking to my house.

"I'm gonna get going." He thumbs over his shoulder, and I see an Uber pulling up. He could've just stayed at the hospital and left from there.

"Okay, sorry about tonight." I walk over to him as Adley becomes limp in my arms, finally losing the battle with sleep.

"No worries."

"Here, I'll take her up," Hudson comes over and takes Adley from me. "I'll put her to bed."

I nod, and although I really want to follow him, I need to talk to Matt. I walk him over to the Uber, and it surprises me when he raises his hands—since we haven't used much sign language tonight. He must want to keep this from Theresa's prying ears.

I'm sorry to leave, but I have to train early in the morning, and I know you want to be with Adley.

I follow his lead and sign back. *Yeah, about...*

He shakes his head. *I know, but I'm going to be selfish and ask you to give me one more chance. An actual uninterrupted date?*

I sigh. *I have a lot on my plate right now.*

He puts one finger up in the air. *Just one date at the lodge.*

Well, I guess now I know what he wants, and it's not a relationship. It's been a long time since I've been with anyone. Maybe a hook-up will get all these annoying thoughts about Hudson and Theresa out of my head. At least Matt will be leaving town soon. *Okay.*

His smile glows under the streetlight. *I'll text you.*

I nod.

He steps forward, kisses me on the cheek, and says in my ear, "Good night, Palmer."

Good night.

He slides into his Uber, and it drives down the street. I turn to head back into the house, but I spot Theresa still standing by Hudson's truck. She's acting as if she wasn't looking at us, but we both know she was. Now I think I know for sure why Matt was signing instead of talking.

"You can come in if you'd like," I tell her on the way to my house.

"No, I'll just wait for Hudson here. I'm sure he won't be long."

I nod and head into my house. I slip off my shoes and shrug off my jacket. As I walk up the stairs, I hear Hudson talking in Adley's room, so I quiet my steps. I'm a sucker when it comes to watching him read Adley a book at night.

"Will you be here in the morning?" Adley asks him. She must have woken up once he tried to put her in bed. She's never been an easy kid to move from one place to another when she's sleeping.

I stand with my back to the wall outside her door.

"No, I'll be at my house, but I'll come over and have some of the donuts your grandma is bringing over if Mommy says it's okay."

"Why can't you sleep with Mommy?"

My hand covers my heart. I hate that we have to explain all this to her.

"Because Mommy and I sleep at our own houses."

"Why? Because of Theresa?"

"We talked about this, Adley. I love Mommy, but not the kind of love that makes us sleep together in the same bed."

I purse my lips to stop myself from laughing.

"I want you to sleep here," she whines.

"I'll tell you what, I'll sleep with you until you fall asleep." I hear some squeaking from him getting on the bed.

"Daddy?"

"Yeah, sweetie."

"Tell me a story."

"What kind of story?" he asks.

"One with Mommy."

"I can do that. So, it was a snowy night, and this

brunette walked into a...an ice cream shop and I was working behind the counter..."

I slide down the wall onto my ass, hearing him tell her a story that's similar to the first time I met him—except this time, the guy buys her the biggest ice cream sundae, and they fall in love like a fairy tale.

Sometimes I wonder what would've happened had we met one another under different circumstances. Would we both be in there with Adley? Would there be no Theresa or Matt? Would we only have one mortgage and raise our daughter as a couple in love?

But those thoughts are useless, so I stand and head downstairs, not wanting the newly raised questions in my head to mess with me. Our life is good. We're good, and whatever this is going on with me, it needs to stop. Hudson and I have a good thing going, and we can't mess that up, no matter how much I might ponder the what-ifs.

thirteen

PALMER

Pete was a perfect gentleman. "Going to a diner" didn't end up being code for his place—he actually pulled into a twenty-four-hour diner just off the main highway. It was called The Rancher's Diner and was a beacon along the dark highway.

Every window in the place was lit up by the fluorescent lights and revealed the sparse sprinkling of people inside. A few people were at the counter, but every red vinyl booth was empty.

Pete got out and held up his finger as he rounded the front of his SUV. He opened Bea's door, and she climbed out with a smile. She tried not to get too excited, but she couldn't stop herself from liking him more and more.

The waitress said a halfhearted hello to them, refilling the coffee of the men scattered along the counter.

Pete put his hand out toward the booths. "Pick one."

Bea went to the booth farthest away from everyone and slid into the bench on the side that sat against the wall. Pete took the bench across from her, picked up the menus hidden behind the condiments, and passed one to Bea. Just as she had admired his hands at the bar, she admired them again. She had no idea what her fascination was about, but his nails were trimmed neatly, and his fingers were long and thin, but not too thin.

She pushed the ridiculousness out of her head. They were hands, everyone had them. There wasn't anything special about Pete's.

"I'm starving." *He lifted the menu and took a cursory glance at it, then put it back down right away.*

Now that they were in the quiet of the diner with the only noise really being the clanking of dishes and the grumbles of old men, she felt self-conscious using her voice. Especially with him. So instead of using her voice, she lifted her hands.

I assume you're a regular?

He laughed, and at that point, she was thankful she'd decided to get cochlear implants just so she could hear that sound.

Instead of talking, he responded in sign language. No. I always get the same thing at any diner. But in all honesty, I was here late one night a few months ago.

He didn't elaborate, and she didn't ask the question she was pretty sure she didn't want the answer to.

What is this dish you always get?

I love breakfast. I get eggs, hash browns, pancakes, bacon. *He chuckled as if it was funny.*

That was a lot of food, but Bea had grown up with brothers who played soccer every minute of their free time, which used tons of energy and burned calories, so she was used to big eaters.

Pancakes do sound good. *Bea looked over the menu, unsure if she wanted breakfast or dinner.* A club sandwich sounds good too.

You get the club, and I'll split my pancakes with you for half of your club?

Sounds perfect.

The waitress came over and took out her pad of paper with a pen, looking as though the last thing she wanted to do was serve them. Pete ordered their food for them, and the waitress left without a word.

This place isn't known for their customer service, but I swear the food makes up for it.

Bea laughed but stopped quickly when she heard her own laughter.

Pete's shoulders sank, and the smile that had been a permanent fixture on his face fell. "Why do you do that?"

Do what? *She knew what he was talking about but decided to play dumb.*

We're signing when you could be talking. *There was a look of genuine concern on Pete's face.*

Instead of answering the question outright, Bea decided to ask a question of her own. Where did you learn to sign?

He sat back in the booth, a look of defeat in his eyes. My dad was deaf.

His admission made Bea relax.

He didn't care for the cochlear implants by the time he got them. So, rarely did he ever use them.

Did he talk? *Bea asked so maybe he could relate.*

When he had to, yes. To get our attention. Honestly, I don't remember it being an issue, but now that you ask, I realize he never talked much outside of the immediate family.

Bea nodded. I got the cochlear implants, and they're great, but I'm still self-conscious.

He reached across the table and took her hand between his. Bea thought her heart might beat out of her chest.

You don't have to feel like that with me. I really like you, and I'd like us to get to know each other better. If you want to do that using sign language, I'm good. You can decide what you're comfortable with.

Bea thought she might faint right there, and then he'd have to call an ambulance. Who was this guy, and how did she get so lucky for their paths to meet?

Okay, I'll give it some thought. Thanks. *She nodded.*

He smiled and shook his head good-naturedly that she was still signing, but luckily, they were interrupted by the food arriving.

One bite had Bea moaning, and Pete's head sprang up to look at her. Something heated was resting between them. She wanted him and she was almost certain he wanted her. All she wanted to do was finish her food and see where he'd take her next. She hoped it was his place.

He dropped his fork and raised his hands. Make noises like that, and we won't finish our meal.

Bea wiped her hands on the napkin. Are you suggesting something? *Finally, we're flirting, Bea thought.*

I'm suggesting that you should eat because you'll need the energy for what I have planned after this.

Her body heated and warmth spread through her veins at the thought of going home with him. Who says I'm going home with you?

He looked her dead in the eyes. Who said anything about my place? I was going to take you paintballing.

Bea's head rocked back, and she laughed out loud despite herself. Pete laughed with her, and the sound filled the entire restaurant. The men on the stools circled around for a moment to look, but Bea didn't care. She was enjoying herself, and that's all there was to it. She knew in that moment that Pete was going to be a part of her life in some capacity.

Two headlights assaulted them through the diner window as a car's tires screeched to a halt in the parking lot. They turned in unison to watch a young woman with a long blonde ponytail get out of the car. She slammed the door and took a bat out of her truck.

"Oh fuck," Pete said, sliding out of the booth.

Bea watched as her heart slipped inch by inch into her stomach. Pete ran outside, and his hand landed on the bat before she could hit the hood of his SUV. She started yelling, and though Bea couldn't tell what they were saying, it was clear that Pete was trying to calm her down. All the old men in the diner had circled around to watch the show, and Bea sat in the booth feeling like an idiot, watching the two of them arguing.

Bea picked up her cell phone and ordered an Uber. She knew better than to think there was something as silly as a soulmate. Whatever she'd felt with Pete was hormones only, and clearly, he probably felt that with a lot of women and then moved on. She'd learned from a young age that men and women do shitty things to one another when they fully give themselves over to someone else. That was the entire reason she'd sworn she'd never get married.

Pete was still arguing with the woman when Bea's Uber arrived. He at least looked back at her once, putting up a finger to say give him a minute while the woman raised her middle finger at Bea and screamed something. But Bea slid out of the booth and slipped into the Uber.

So much for Prince Charming and happily ever afters, Bea thought as she drove away.

Another chapter done. God, that felt good. I shut my laptop and put it in my bag. Since Adley's fall, I want to be with her every minute, so although I should be writing, I'm picking her up and taking her to Sweet Suga Things.

I'm just about out of the cabin when my phone vibrates. *Hudson.*

As much time as I've been trying to spend time with Adley, I've been dodging Hudson. The night of the accident, he came downstairs after she'd fallen asleep, and I tried to act normal. As if we hadn't fought and these weird thoughts about him weren't filling my head. As if I didn't know that his girlfriend was waiting for him outside.

I waved from the couch, and he wavered, probably wanting to talk about our argument, until I told him that Theresa was waiting outside because she didn't want to come in. He left my place. Eventually, Theresa drove off, and he went into his house. I sat on the couch wondering what had changed between us. Where were these feelings coming from?

I'm out anyway so I can get Adley.

Usually, I'd take him up on the offer, but I'm already outside of the cabin.

I'm happy to. Going to take her out.

What about your deadline?

I'm taking a break to get her.

Want to go wherever you're going with her together?

I bite my cheek. That idea is probably trouble, but he'll find it odd if I say no.

Sure. Meet us at Sweet Suga Things.

This morning from your mom AND this afternoon? You're spoiling her.

I'm sure you were going to do the same thing.

I was. LOL See you there.

I put my phone in my bag, lock up the cabin, and climb into my SUV.

Adley is all smiles when she sees me, and I tell her we're going for a surprise.

By the time we park, and I place her on the sidewalk, Hudson is waiting outside Sweet Suga Things. He's come right from the slopes, his messy helmet hair a sure giveaway.

He really is sexy. Sometimes I forget how badly I wanted him that first night we met.

"Look, Daddy!" I point in his direction, and Adley runs toward him.

His jeans are slung a little low, and his puffy jacket is open, revealing his sweatshirt that's so faded you can barely read the ski destination he got it from. It's his smile that captures me though, causing me to quicken my footsteps.

Adley runs right into his arms, and he picks her up, swinging her around in a circle. She screams in excitement, and he laughs. Why is that laugh having the same effect on me it did once upon a time? I've heard it a million times over the years without feeling this way.

"Who wants a sugar high?" he asks Adley.

She raises her hand. "Me! I do!"

He lowers her to the ground. "Then go tell Miss Greta

what you want." He opens the door, and she runs inside, her hands and nose soon glued to the cookie case.

"You just gave her the key to the vault," I say, walking through the door he's holding open.

"After that scare, I'll buy her the entire bakery."

I shake my head, and he comes in right behind me, his cologne wafting around us.

Damn him.

I turn to face him and sign, *I'm going to the bathroom.* I turn away, and he places his hand in mine. Electricity shoots up my arm. I tear it away, and he draws back.

He looks at me in confusion. "I was just going to ask you what you want."

"Um..." I stare at the cases and cases of sugary goodness. I raise my hands. *Cookie please.*

"Okay."

He studies me for a beat, but I quickly turn around and disappear down the hallway to the bathroom. I lock the door and rest my back against it.

Get a grip, Palmer. He's your best friend and the father of your child. Not someone you can sleep with to get it out of your system.

I dig my phone from my purse, needing an outlet.

> When did you want to have that date? I have tomorrow night open.

> Pick you up at six?

> Perfect.

I shove the phone in my bag and stare at myself in the mirror.

This is the right decision even if my gut says it's not.

PALMER

I'm surprised I didn't get a speeding ticket on the way over to the cabin. The minute I get in, I toss my bag on the chair, sit on the couch with my laptop, and my fingers can't catch up to my thoughts as I type.

Nia burst into Bea's room, jumped on the bed, and shook her awake. Bea shot up, alarmed that maybe there was a fire or a break-in.

"What?" she asked, her body in full alarm panic.

Nia waited while Bea sat up and put on her cochlear implants.

"What happened last night?" Nia lay down on the bed. "Because there's a hot bartender in the living room with breakfast for you."

Bea replayed the night before. Had her taking an Uber home alone been a dream? She looked down at herself. Not naked, pajamas on. She'd thought it was going somewhere with Pete, but then that blonde girl showed up. How did he even know where she lived?

"What?" Bea asked again to make sure she'd heard her friend correctly.

"The bartender from last night...when I got home, he was sitting outside the apartment."

"When did you get home?" Bea rubbed the sleep from my eyes. She had slept hard, so she wasn't surprised she hadn't seen the strobing light if he'd rung the doorbell. But the more important question was, why was he here?

"Just now." Her smile suggested she'd done the walk of shame from wherever she and Trek had ended up the night before. Bea was just thankful it wasn't at their place. "Now... go."

Bea glanced down at herself once more. She was wearing boxer shorts and a Weezer T-shirt that was so threadbare Pete would be able to see her nipples. "Um..."

Nia saw the worried expression and sprang up from the bed. She was so hyper and in such a good mood, the sex with Trek must have been great. "I'll stall while you get yourself together."

She was out of Bea's room before Bea could explain what happened last night and tell her to kick Pete out.

That left her having to face him, so she grabbed a sweatshirt off the back of the chair and went into her bathroom. She brushed her teeth, and finger-combed her hair into a messy bun. Why was she even putting in any effort? The guy was a douche, and it was creepy that he had somehow found out where she lived. She didn't need to impress him.

She opened her bedroom door, and Pete's laugh rang out, the one that had made her all tingly, and damn it all to hell, that same feeling rushed back between her thighs again. Damn him.

His gaze caught hers when she stepped out from the short

hallway where the bedrooms were. He stood as if they were going to go somewhere.

Bea opened her mouth, but Pete raised his hand. "Give me a chance to explain."

She nodded and sat in the chair farthest away from him.

He raised a white plastic bag with what seemed to be a few Styrofoam containers in it. "I picked up some pancakes for breakfast."

She didn't say anything, just crossed her arms and waited.

"Sarah is an ex."

She raised her eyebrows with an expression as if to say, "Duh."

"We've been over for a while, but she doesn't want to accept it." He appeared nervous, as though he cared what Bea thought. "I swear we're not together."

Bea nodded. She wouldn't deny that she had hang-ups about relationships. Getting serious with anyone seemed to come as a struggle. Finding out about her parents' early years when she was fourteen years old had messed her up, even though her parents were blissfully happy now. She wanted to believe in true love and soulmates, but all she could think was that Pete had baggage. Baggage she didn't want to carry the weight of. Baggage was what had torn her parents apart when she wasn't even born yet.

She raised her hands. You don't owe me an explanation.

He looked at his feet and back up. "I like you, Bea."

He appeared earnest and genuine.

"Why?" she asked before shaking her head. "Never mind. We only met last night."

"I know, but you feel it, right?"

This was her moment to say no, she didn't feel anything. To say that he was just like any other guy she'd met at a bar, but he'd know she was lying. There was something between them. Something she wished she could explain. It would make it a lot easier to kick him out right now.

She shrugged, unable to say it verbally because then it would be out in the universe.

Pete stared at her long and hard, and she knew he saw the truth of it. His lips turned down and his teeth pinned down his bottom lip. She felt him almost silently asking her, "You're really not going to see what we could be?"

The image of Sarah flying into the parking lot of the diner came to her again. She must be tracking him somehow to know where they were. Bea didn't want that drama in her life. As attracted as she was to Pete, she couldn't willingly invite that into her life. Not to mention if Sarah was still so attached to Pete, Bea would probably become just as attached, and then what would happen to her after he broke her heart? What if he changed his mind and decided Sarah was the one he wanted?

"Then can we at least be friends?"

Her gaze flew up to meet his, surprised by his request. How was she going to be friends with him when all she wanted was to have sex with him?

"Get to know me better. Find out that you can trust me."

Her forehead crinkled. She didn't understand why this was so important to him, but she did enjoy his company. Friends wasn't a horrible thing. From what she'd gathered from the conversations they'd had, he seemed like he wanted to see the world and didn't want to stay in one place for too long. He loved snowboarding and was trying to get to every big ski resort he could.

Nia's head popped out of the kitchen behind Pete. So, she had been eavesdropping the entire time. Great. Her eyes went wide, and she gestured that Bea should say yes.

What did she have to lose? He'd probably be gone soon, and Bea would never see him again anyway. "Sure."

He smiled and grabbed the plastic bag, pulling it toward him. "Do you have any syrup?"

She stared at him as though he was one zoo animal humping another one. She finally asked the question that had been bothering her. "How did you find me?"

"It's a small town. Jared is a friend."

Jared? Bea tried to figure out if that name was familiar, then it came to her. "My Uber driver?"

Pete sheepishly smiled and nodded, opening up the container of pancakes. He probably hoped the distraction of the fluffy goodness would override the revelation of Jared's invasion of privacy.

Bea went to the kitchen to grab the syrup. She didn't know how she'd push away her sexual feelings toward Pete in order to be just his friend, but that he'd gone to this much trouble to apologize to her meant something in her book.

One year later...

Bea was at the end of the bar, where most of her Friday nights were now spent. Usually, Pete served, and she would sit there with the small group of friends that congregated there every Friday night. But Pete had tonight off, and they were celebrating Nia's engagement to Trek. Turned out Pete and Bea were both wrong. Trek was head over heels in love with Nia and had popped the question the night before, and Nia had ecstatically accepted.

Bea had watched them fall more and more in love for the past year. Trek had even asked Bea to go with him to pick out the ring. She couldn't believe that this guy who had been such a womanizer had changed all because of one girl. Of course, her best friend was awesome, and he would've been crazy not to see that the day Nia came into his life had been the best day of his, but it went against everything Bea believed. Trek had changed all because of Nia. As hard as she tried, Bea couldn't wrap her head around the idea.

Tonight, they were celebrating. Trek was already drunk but kept pestering Dimitri for more shots. And Trek didn't take all the shots on his own. He ordered for everyone. Trek wasn't only celebrating his new wife-to-be tonight. After Bea had gotten to know him, she had agreed to send his band's music to her well-known music producer uncle. He had got it into the right hands, and Trek's band had signed with a label a month ago. They were moving to Los Angeles, and Trek was taking Nia with him. Which left Bea without a roommate, but thankfully Pete was moving in.

She and Pete had remained friends throughout the past year, and although there were a few times Bea had thought it might lead to more, she couldn't pull the trigger. Pete was an intricate part of her life now, and if something went bad, she didn't know what would happen. Would she be Sarah, driving erratically into a diner parking lot, baseball bat in hand to do damage to his SUV? Plus, now he was going to be her roommate, so they definitely couldn't cross the line.

"Let's go, Bea, drink the shot." Trek put his arm around her shoulders. "I owe you the world."

Bea shook her head. She was surprised by how fond she was of Trek now. He treated Nia like a princess, and Bea had witnessed him deny girl after girl since they'd gotten together, telling them all that he was taken. She knew Nia would be in good hands with him.

"I've drank enough," Bea said loudly because she was already buzzed.

"You're getting drunk with me."

"Hate to break it to you, but you're already drunk," Bea said into his ear.

"Because life is good." He grabbed Nia. "I got my girl. I got my band. We got FUCKING SIGNED!"

He pulled Nia onto the dance floor, and Bea was thankful she didn't have to drink another shot. Pete tugged on Bea's arm, and she fell down next to him in the booth. His eyes were glassy, and he had on his goofy drunk smile.

"Hey, roomie," he said and put his arm around her. "Let's toast." He pushed a shot glass her way and lifted his.

She raised the glass and clinked Pete's, but she didn't drink the shot. Instead, she placed it back on the table.

"Oh, no, no." Pete held it up for her. "You're going to give us bad juju if you don't drink."

"Juju?" Bea questioned, laughing at Pete. She rarely saw him lose control of himself like he had tonight. She kind of liked that she'd be taking care of him tonight instead of the reverse. This year had proved one thing—Pete was a natural caregiver. He'd brought her soup when she was sick, chocolates when she was PMSing, and pancakes when she was hungover. They'd shared a love for horror movies during the month of October, county festivals in the summer, and recently joined a dart league at the bar Pete worked at on Thursday nights.

"Just drink." He pushed it closer.

She finally took the shot glass and downed the shot, then smiled at Pete. "Happy?"

"Not really. Get drunk with me." Pete grabbed a pitcher to refill his beer and sloppily poured it into her half-empty glass until it was full again.

Bea knew Trek was now the least of her worries. She'd have to get Pete home as well.

Before she could answer, Pete nudged her with his hip to get out of the booth, took her hand, and led her to the dance floor.

"Should I Stay or Should I Go" by The Clash was play-

ing, and Pete and Trek sang along, their hands in the air as they jumped up and down.

Nia rolled her eyes but laughed. Then the four of them danced and laughed together. Pete spun her out and dragged her back to him. He kept singing the lyrics, his face in Bea's the majority of the time.

Something happened after that dance. More drinks were brought to the dance floor by Trek's bandmates. More alcohol was consumed, and they sweated through their clothes, dancing and making complete fools of themselves.

At the end of the night when it was time to go home, Bea and Pete were thrown into an Uber together.

"Jared!" Pete said with a smile once they were secure in the back seat, and he saw who their driver was.

Bea and Pete looked at each other and laughed the entire way back to the apartment. Bea couldn't remember a time when she'd had so much fun.

HUDSON

Matt doesn't really need me anymore. He's figured out his kinks by now, but he's paying me, so I show up on the halfpipe, give him a couple of things to work on, then we usually end up heading to the slopes to shred a few runs or to the lodge for a drink.

"I'm exhausted," he says after his fifth run. He lies down on the top of the hill as we stare down at the halfpipe. "You should go for a rip. When's the last time you rode the halfpipe?"

I don't deny it's tempting. Watching the young kids trying shit and the excitement when they land a trick makes me envious, but then I think about Adley. And I think about not seeing her grow up because of something stupid I did. "Nah."

"Hey, Matt," two women say in unison, waving at him as their eyes eat him up.

He just gives them a halfhearted wave. "Either I'm getting way too fucking old, or women these days are looking a lot fucking younger." His gaze follows the women as they put their snowboards in the snow and sit to watch people on the halfpipe.

"It's called jailbait, and you are old."

He tosses some snow at me. "I remember when I was just coming up, and Grady Kale was the old fucker at the Winter Games in Korea."

I nod, remembering. Although Matt is just as cocky as he was then, he's matured a lot. But I think every kid as good as Matt, especially at such a young age, is cocky to a degree. They earned their right to be. And I think you need to be in order to launch yourself toward danger at the top of the mountain. You have to believe you can pull it off.

"Now you're the Grady, and there are younger versions of you." I gesture toward the halfpipe.

"Truth." He stares at the guys and girls who are more than a decade younger than him. "It's sad as fuck."

"It's not bad, you know."

He glances at me as though he doesn't know what I'm referring to.

"Stability. Domestic life as you refer to it. There's a peace to growing roots." I can't believe I'm actually admitting it since I never wanted to settle down in one place. Not once in my life. Even if I met someone, I'd hoped they'd want to travel the world like I did.

Matt shakes his head. "You've been brainwashed."

I realize there's no getting through to Matt. He's lived the lifestyle longer than I ever did, and maybe if Palmer had never gotten pregnant, I'd be telling some other guy the same thing Matt is telling me.

"But I'll tell you one thing, Palmer is great," Matt says. "She's so easygoing. You hit the jackpot as far as baby mamas go."

If he only knew how high-strung Palmer can be about

certain things. He's never seen her lose her shit. Being a parent can do that to you. Like when Adley was an infant, and she wouldn't sleep for multiple nights, or when we tried to wean her off the pacifier, or when we potty trained her.

I never knew how much patience being a parent required, and sometimes you just need a time-out. But Matt wouldn't know anything about that. And if I'm honest with myself, I like it when Palmer gets a little crazy and needs a break because I like being her Superman and swooping in to save the day. I'm sure to some people that sounds bad, but it goes both ways. I lose my shit too, and she's always the one to help me.

"Yeah, she's great," I say.

"I have to ask again because we're going on a date tonight, and I just...I can't shake the feeling that I'm inter-fering, getting myself in the middle of something. That maybe there's more between you two?" He arches an eyebrow.

This is my chance to tell him to back off. That since he entered the picture, I've become a jealous bastard and am currently blowing up my own relationship because I'm hyper-focused on the two of them. But Palmer's not mine, and I can't take this away from her. Plus, there's still Theresa to consider.

"Nah, man, it's cool." He studies me for a beat, and I play off my discomfort with a laugh. "I swear, it's cool."

"All right, then tell me where to take her. Someone at the hotel told me some restaurant named Terra and Mare downtown is the one to go to?"

I forgot that Matt has no idea who Palmer is in this town. If he ever planned to stay long term, he'd learn what her family means to this town and all the different hands that would be in their relationship. I don't even realize I'm laughing until Matt speaks again.

"Is it a shit place?" he asks, not understanding.

"It's her uncle's restaurant. Go there, and you'll be in Buzz Wheel that night and be inundated with her family members wanting to know what's going on."

"Seriously? At Glacier Point, the owner came up to me, and when I said I was here to train with you, he said he was Palmer's uncle too."

"She's got a lot of aunts and uncles plus over twenty cousins. Most of them live in Lake Starlight for at least part of the year. Her one cousin is Easton Bailey."

His eyes widen. "The Chicago Colts player?"

I nod. "Plus, another cousin married that professional soccer player, Rylan Greene. His family is from Sunrise Bay, the next town over."

He sits up straight and shakes his head. Matt's a big deal, especially in the snowboarding arena, but the Winter Games are only every four years, so he's not nearly as well-known as Palmer's cousins. I don't mention the fact that her mom's twin is the famous singer Phoenix Bailey and her husband, Griffin, is an esteemed music producer.

"Damn. That's impressive. No wonder she doesn't get all googly-eyed like so many other women around me."

That comment right there makes me suspicious. Is Matt only pursuing Palmer because she's not fawning all over him?

"I feel like I really need to make sure this is a good date now. Maybe we should go to Anchorage."

I nod. "You're safer there than anywhere around here. Even Winterberry Falls has informants who will gossip about you guys to Buzz Wheel."

"What the hell is this Buzz Wheel?"

I take off my gloves, dig into my pocket, and pull out my phone. "It's an app that posts the town gossip. Anyone who's a Bailey is always in there, along with other people in town. No one knows who writes it. It used to be an online blog that would erase each entry after twenty-four hours, but now that it's an app, you can read any article you want."

"Fucking small towns." He hands me back my phone.

I nod and put it back in my pocket, zip it closed, and pull on my gloves.

"One more run and I'm done." He gets up and walks over to the top of the halfpipe where he takes the liberty of going ahead of everyone.

I get on my board and make my way down the hill to meet him at the bottom. I hate the fact Matt's going to be alone with her tonight. I know Palmer—she might even sleep with him. Fuck, the image of Matt having his hands on her, grinding inside of her, kissing her skin is agonizing.

Jesus. I slide to a stop at the bottom of the hill. I'm in so deep, I don't know how to climb my way out. Where is all this coming from? Jealousy isn't my thing. It never has been.

Damn it all to hell. I might need an exorcism.

I WALK into Palmer's house later that day. "Hello!"

"Up here," a voice other than Palmer's calls.

I groan because I recognize that voice, and this one's always giving me shit.

I climb the stairs and follow the sound of laughter to Palmer's bedroom. Adley is lying on the bed, enthralled with some television show.

"Hey, kiddo," I say, sitting next to her.

"Daddy!" She climbs into my lap but continues watching television, leaning her head against my chest.

Harper is curling Palmer's hair while she sits in a chair facing her vanity mirror, watching.

"What's all this?" I motion to the two of them. I know, but I want Palmer to tell me.

"Don't you know, my cousin has a hot D-A-T-E with a snowboarder." Harper waggles her eyebrows.

At least she spelled out the word date. I'm assuming for Adley's benefit.

"The other day it looked like you wanted to be the one out with the snowboarder."

Harper glares at me with the curling iron still in Palmer's hair.

"Harp!"

"Shit. Sorry." She quickly loosens the barrel and pulls it from Palmer's hair.

"Now you swear in front of my kid?" I say, arching an eyebrow.

Harper and I have a unique relationship. She's the classic feisty redhead who speaks her mind about everything. And usually, when I'm alone with her, she's telling me that I'm an idiot and saying cliché things like, "shit or get off the pot" or "fish or cut bait." I'm not sure Harper would be capable of being only friends with a guy. She's the horniest woman I've ever met. She's always talking about sex or men or her hookups. That's not a judgment. She's single and an adult, she can do what she wants. But I think to her, Palmer and I are like a rare species she just can't wrap her head around.

"Like you don't ever swear." Harper rolls her eyes and continues curling Palmer's hair.

I can tell Palmer is reading our lips in the reflection of the mirror because her cochlear implants aren't in. Through the mirror, she signs to both of us. *Cut it out.*

Harper stares at her in the mirror. "Why? It's fun getting him all riled up. What was he like in bed?" she whispers the last part so Adley won't hear, but she isn't paying us any attention anyway.

Palmer rolls her eyes. *Missionary only and doesn't go down.*

Harper balks and turns around to stare at me.

Fuck off. I sign at them both.

Palmer laughs, knowing it's not true. Hell, lately I've been beating off to the few moments of that night that I remember, plus I've filled in the blanks with some of my own imagination.

Harper puts down the curling iron and sprays Palmer's hair with an obnoxious amount of hairspray. Palmer stands and takes the towel off her shoulders, and it's then I see that she's wearing a dress.

A dress?

Palmer doesn't wear dresses. At least not unless it's a wedding or something. She's a jeans-and-T-shirt girl, shorts in the summer. Most of the time when she does have to dress up, she wears pants. A dress makes things especially accessible. Only one slide of the hand up her leg, and you're inches from her core.

Panic rises inside me, making my chest tight. Matt will take advantage of this dress.

"You're wearing a dress?" I ask since she's facing me.

She looks puzzled then walks to her closet, her bare leg sliding out from the fabric.

Fucking hell, there's a slit. In the dress.

"Yes, she's wearing a dress. I picked it out. It looks great on her, doesn't it?" Harper gives me a shit-eating grin.

I squint at her. Of course she'd choose a dress for Palmer. All you have to do is straddle a guy and slide the underwear to the side and bingo. Harper's right that Palmer looks hot as hell though. I haven't seen Palmer this done up in a while. She's had back-to-back deadlines for the past year, and the book she's working on now has taken a lot out of her. Not that she isn't gorgeous in her sweats and sweatshirts with her hair thrown up in a messy bun, but this is a showstopper, and Matt's going to love it.

What are you doing tonight? Palmer signs then grabs her boots. At least they will cover up part of her legs.

She sits next to me on the bed, and her perfume smells delicious. I want it all over me after a night with her. I want to smell it the next day on my sheets.

Wait. What the hell was that?

"Theresa is coming over. I can take Adley," I say, my voice a bit strained.

Adley sits up straight. "No, Daddy. Harper. We're making cupcakes."

"I can make cupcakes too."

Palmer shakes her head and raises her hands. *You and Theresa need time together. I saw her at the hospital, and you're going to lose her if you don't put the effort in.*

I'm not surprised that she saw Theresa's pissed-off expression. She notices everything Theresa does.

Palmer grabs her cochlear implants from the vanity she was sitting in front of and puts them on.

"Plus, Adley wants me to babysit her." Harper holds out her hands and Adley scoots across the mattress over to her. "Right?"

"Right!" Adley screams.

Palmer laughs. "Don't burn down the kitchen," she says while signing.

The doorbell rings, and Harper turns so Adley can climb onto her back.

"We'll get it because you're going to make a grand entrance," she says to Palmer.

Harper and my daughter leave the room, leaving me alone with Palmer. She bends down in front of the mirror, fixing her makeup.

"Don't go," I blurt before I can think better of it, and Palmer stills.

sixteen

HUDSON

Palmer turns around and stares at me as though I just told her a meteor is about to fall from the sky and kill us all. Her expression holds shock, surprise, and a hint of fight-or-flight mode. "What?"

"Don't go." I rise off the bed and take her hands. "Don't go out with Matt."

Her face relaxes, and a small sigh slips from her lips. She speaks out loud since Adley is no longer in the room. "Hudson, I know this is different, I haven't dated anyone in a while, but you have nothing to worry about. Matt is a fling. We both know he's not going to stick around here. Nothing is going to change with how we parent Adley."

Awesome. So she's basically telling me she's only going out with him to sleep with him. Perfect. Jealousy is like a monster clawing inside my chest.

"That's not what I mean. Fuck." I walk away, pushing my fingers through my hair. How do I explain this to her when I'm not even sure I understand what's going on myself?

"Palm! Someone is here for you!" Harper screams up the

stairs.

Palmer turns and inspects herself in the mirror one last time. She walks toward the door, and I reach it before she does, shutting it before she can escape.

She comes to an abrupt stop, forehead wrinkled. "Hudson, what's going on?"

I shake my head. "Give me a minute."

"We can talk about this when I get home." She reaches for the doorknob, but I shift my body in front of the door.

"No."

"What is wrong with you?" She crosses her arms, giving me the look she used to when we'd fight over something to do with Adley.

I pinch the bridge of my nose. "All my thoughts are just jumbled right now."

As I say that, Theresa pops into my head. How can I tell Palmer not to go out with Matt when I have Theresa on her way over for our own date?

"I just don't want you to go."

"Is there something wrong with Matt? Is he going to murder me? Does he have, like, eight different baby mamas and doesn't pay child support?" Her head tilts to the side.

"No. None of that." Matt's a great guy. He's not looking for anything serious, but now I see that Palmer really isn't either, so it cancels itself out.

"Then I don't understand where this is coming from."

She's right. From her perspective, this is all coming out of left field. As all these feelings have resurfaced inside me, she's been living the life we created—a lifelong friendship and co-parenting agreement. Hell, she's watched me with Theresa for months and even warned me that Theresa is looking to get serious. Never once has Palmer ever acted jealous.

Fuck. I'm alone in this. If I stop her from going out with Matt, I'm an asshole because what I'm feeling, she isn't.

"Never mind." I step away from the door, but she doesn't reach for the knob.

"Hudson?"

I look up, and damn, I hate the fact she's so done up for another man. "Nothing. Sorry."

Palmer doesn't move, watching me, waiting for me to fill her in. She's my best friend, and I don't think she's seen me this nervous since the time I went to her house after the first night we met. I'd been prepared for her to kick me in the balls and send me on my way.

"Honestly." I open the door, my gut churning. "Go enjoy your night."

Her gaze doesn't leave me because she's probably worried I need medical attention at this point. "Are you sure?"

"Yeah. You look great. Go."

Staring at me the entire time, she slowly walks through the doorway. I don't stop her because how will it affect us if I open my chest and let my heart out into her hands, and she doesn't accept it? Then it will be awkward and weird, and we're going to be in each other's lives until the end of one of ours.

I follow her down the stairs. Matt tilts his head when he sees me following her.

Adley sits on the couch watching her favorite movie about characters that are elements falling in love. I shouldn't be surprised she loves a movie that's romance-based. Her mom is the same.

My attention falls to Adley's lap, then shifts to Harper. Adley has an entire bowl of microwave popcorn in her lap.

Her butter-covered fingers dig into the bowl, then push a handful of kernels into her mouth.

"Adley, be careful, you'll choke," I say.

Harper laughs. "So overprotective." She thumbs in my direction, looking at Matt as if he doesn't know who she's talking about.

"Why don't you give her a small bowl?"

"Hey, it's my night with her. I'm the babysitter. You go do whatever you're doing. Go do Theresa."

"Yes, you're the babysitter, not the parent. There are rules babysitters have to adhere to." My gaze shifts to Palmer. Matt's hands are on the small of her back. They're hugging. Who hugs at the start of a date?

"I think I hear Theresa calling you," Harper says, putting her hand on the outside of her ear. "She says she'll do anal if you hurry."

"Harper!" Palmer turns to her with wide eyes.

At least she's out of Matt's arms now. Never thought I'd thank Harper for anything.

Harper covers Adley's ears. "She isn't paying attention, and she doesn't know what anal means."

"So you say it twice." I frown and shake my head.

"I covered her ears."

"And that solves the problem?"

"Okay, we're heading out," Palmer says while signing.

"Hey, man." Matt fist bumps me then scurries after Palmer, placing his hand on the small of her back to guide her out the front door.

I don't realize I'm watching them through the window until a throat clears behind me.

Stripping my gaze away, I find Harper laughing on the couch. Adley stares at her as if she's crazy—probably because the movie isn't at a funny part.

Disregarding Adley, Harper stands and pats me on the back. "I give you a lot of credit."

"Why?"

"I'm not sure I could watch it all like you are," she says, walking toward the kitchen.

"Watch what?" I follow her.

"Watch the person you want to be with leave with another man. A man she's probably going to fuck tonight. A man she'll probably get naked with and let him lick her entire body."

I choke on the bile rising up my throat. "You have such a way with words, Harper. How come you're not a writer too?" I grumble.

She shrugs. "I'm just saying. You're losing the best thing in your life."

I turn to look through the window at the driveway again, but all I see is Matt's rental drive off with Palmer in it. Am I so transparent that Harper sees what's eating me up inside?

"You don't know what you're talking about."

She grabs a water and leans against the fridge. "Okay then."

I want to bombard her with questions about whether she thinks Palmer wants me too. If we've been stupid all these years, keeping a friendship alive when we could be so much more. But movement in my peripheral has me turning to see Theresa pulling into my driveway.

My heart sinks.

"Let Theresa suck you off, and maybe it will make you forget everything until Palmer returns." Harper smiles widely at me and disappears into the family room.

I flip her off, but unfortunately, she doesn't see it.

I walk out of Palmer's house through the back door as

usual, and Theresa's smile drops when she sees me.

It's at that moment that I realize that something has to be done. Something I don't look forward to doing, but it's not fair to Theresa no matter what happens with Palmer and me. Theresa can't be stuck in the middle while I try to figure out what the hell it is that these newfound feelings for Palmer mean.

Crossing the driveway, my stomach turns over. I hate hurting people. I never would've pursued Theresa if I knew these feelings for Palmer were still festering, lying dormant all these years.

"Hey." She thumbs over her shoulder. "I think I just passed Matt and Palmer."

"What do you have there?" I ask, ignoring the Matt and Palmer topic and inquiring about the two grocery bags in her hand. Thinking about Palmer on her date agitates me, and if I'm going to break up with Theresa, I don't want it to be on bad terms because I was in a shit mood when I did it.

Lake Starlight is a small town, and although maybe I don't know everyone, I don't want Adley to hear one day what a jerk her dad is.

"Dinner!" Theresa seems oddly happy, almost as though it's fake. "And I'm making your favorite. Beef tenderloin and my mushroom sauce."

Fuck. I love that dish. Guilt races up my spine. I cannot let her go to all the effort of cooking me my favorite dish and then breaking this off. She walks ahead of me to go into the house. I haven't broken up with anyone since my crazy ex with the baseball bat, and I don't want a repeat of that experience. Since her, I only had flings. Women I never saw more than a few times and never wanted a future with.

I follow Theresa into the house and catch her throwing away the orange chicken I just got for lunch yesterday. Then

I watch as she places pre-made salads in the fridge along with some yogurt.

Watching her, I rethink our time together and whether my feelings for Palmer are just from jealousy or some weird alpha male protectiveness. Is this a rash decision? Theresa could make dinner and spend the night for me to test this theory, so I don't end up throwing away something I'll miss later on.

But something in my gut tells me I'm only making excuses. Besides, I'm not one of those dicks who string women along.

"I think we need to talk," I say, shocked that I'm so blunt.

Theresa turns and looks at me, her face sinking. It confirms that she's not surprised it's come to this. She knows what I'm about to say.

She shuts the fridge and keeps her distance on the other side of the room. "About?"

"Us."

She nods. "What about us?" Her tone turns almost sarcastic.

"I'm not sure...I mean..."

"Spit it out, Hudson." She crosses her arms, and her eyes narrow. She's pissed.

"If you know what I'm going to say, then why do you need me to say it?"

"Because I want to hear the words from your mouth."

I look at the floor then back up at her. "I think we should break up." God, how junior high does that sound? I clear my throat. "I mean, things have changed."

"Not for me. I still love you."

Love? My heart skitters, and not in a good way. She loves me? When did love enter the equation?

"Don't look so alarmed. It's a natural emotion when you're dating someone."

Okay, it's clear to me that we're not going to end this on good terms.

"I just didn't think we were there yet. You caught me by surprise."

Her arms drop, and her shoulders rise and fall in a deep sigh. "No, Hudson, you weren't there yet because you're too afraid to commit to someone." I open my mouth to respond, but she's not finished. "If you could commit to someone, you would've done so with Palmer when you got her pregnant. Or hell, maybe earlier."

She has no idea what my past with Palmer entails, that it was Palmer who kept us as friends in the beginning, not me.

"I'm sorry," I say, not knowing what else to say to smooth this over.

"Sorry? I'm so sick of men. Men like you. Men who just flit around and mess with women's hearts and then move on. I should've known." She circles back to the fridge, shoving the things she bought back in her grocery bags. "You're just scared." She flips around and grabs her purse, shoving it on her shoulder. "Grow up, Hudson."

"Can't we talk about this? Be civil."

Her mouth drops. Guess that was the wrong thing to say.

"Civil about what? That you want to break up with me because you've developed feelings for your baby mama?"

My head rears back. "I never said anything about Palmer."

A condescending laugh erupts out of her, but she quickly sobers. "Do you think I'm stupid? I knew from the get-go that your situation isn't normal. Living side by side, the constant going in and out of one another's home. The hugging, the inside jokes when you use sign language with each other. All the signs were there, but I was the stupid one who ignored them."

"We're just friends raising our baby." I'm telling her the truth, but she'll never believe I didn't realize my feelings had changed until recently. When Matt came into town and threatened to steal her away from me.

"And now?" She puts her hand on her hip and cocks it.

I'm not going to tell her anything before I even divulge what I'm feeling to Palmer. "Listen, I'm trying to be nice about this. I just think we're looking for two different things here."

She laughs, one that suggests I'm unbelievable. "Yeah, I want you, and you want your baby mama. So, let me get out of your hair so you can go track her down." She storms over to the back door.

"Can't we be adults about this?"

She whips around, and there's pure venom in her eyes. There's a long silence, and my gaze shifts to the knives in the block on the counter, wondering if she's about to make a mad dash for one.

"Goodbye, Hudson. Have a great life. If you see me around, do us both a favor and ignore me." She walks out, slamming the door behind her.

Well, I obviously fucked that up.

She pulls out of the driveway, tires squealing in pure heartbroken teenage girl fashion. I feel like a complete shit.

I blink, realizing that even though what I just did sucks, it feels right. I need to find Palmer and confess my feelings before she does something with Matt, but I have no idea where they're going.

I run next door and barge through the door. Harper and

Adley are sitting on the floor in the family room while Harper paints Adley's nails.

"Daddy!" Adley holds up her hand. "Pink."

"Those look pretty." I give her a smile then turn my attention to Harper.

Harper holds the nail polish mid swipe on Adley's other hand, staring up at me. "Are you training for a marathon? Why do you look so flushed?"

"Did Palmer say where they were going?" I ask as nonchalantly as possible.

She turns back to Adley and continues to paint her nails, but I don't miss the smile she's trying to fight. "Why?"

I decide to cut the shit. "Harper, you know why, so just tell me."

The movie is still on the TV while Harper does her nails, so thankfully it grabs Adley's attention away from our conversation.

"Finally biting the bullet?" Harper asks.

"Harper." I can barely hold any niceness in my tone.

She laughs. "Glacier Point Resort. Eating, and well, you know what else."

Shit. I have to get there before she sleeps with him.

I bend down and kiss Adley on the cheek.

"Daddy?" She turns her head to watch her movie.

As I head toward the door, Harper calls, "A thank you would be nice."

Turning around, I peek my head into the family room. "Thanks."

She smiles at me, one that's too sweet for Harper, and says, "You're welcome."

I run out to my truck, put the key in the ignition, then my own tires are squealing when I put the truck in reverse.

seventeen

PALMER

Matt's been a perfect gentleman. He's been kind and sweet and nothing like I assumed he would be. I figured he might be a tad egotistical because he's likely used to getting what he wants. Which I hope includes me at least for tonight. But he's been gracious and almost humble as people approach him while we walk through the entrance of the Glacier Point Resort and head to their restaurant.

When he mentioned coming here, I didn't want to tell him my uncle owns it, so I wait patiently as he talks to the hostess about the fact that we don't have a reservation.

I see him try to slyly hand her some cash, but the young girl opens her hand and stares at the one-hundred-dollar bill as though it's a fossil. I guess young people aren't used to being bribed for a good table these days.

I wish my thoughts were on this date and how good-looking Matt is, but they're back in my bedroom with Hudson. Why was he acting so strange? He hasn't been that flustered around me since the morning after the night we met, when he showed up at my apartment. It was as if he was scared how I was going to react to whatever he wanted to tell me.

"I'm Matt Peterson," he whispers, and the doe-eyed teenage girl stares with a blank expression. Then he glances at me with a sheepish expression. "It's all booked."

I nod and step up to the stand. I smile sweetly, lean closer, and say, "I'm Palmer Ferguson, Wyatt Whitmore's niece."

Her eyes widen, and her head swivels right and left, as if my uncle is going to pop up out of nowhere. "Oh, I'm sorry. Let me get someone to help." She scurries off before I have a chance to tell her it's not a 9-1-1 situation.

"You've got more clout than me here." Matt laughs. "And she pocketed my Benjamin anyway."

"I'm not sure if Hudson told you—"

"That your family owns the majority of Lake Starlight? Yeah, he mentioned it. Plus, your rock star aunt, Phoenix, and your all-star cousin, Easton. You come from a good gene pool."

I shake my head and smile. "I think there's just so many of us. Some were bound to become bigger names than others."

"I'm the only one from my entire town who made it big, so I'm not sure that's the correct theory."

The hostess comes back to the stand and grabs two menus. "We have the chef's table in the kitchen open."

Even Matt's eyebrows raise. "Wow."

Our meal will be comped, that much I know, so I hope Matt isn't worried about what this will cost.

Matt holds his arm out for me to go first, and I follow the young girl through packed tables holding loud conversations, then through a door to the even louder kitchen. People are yelling, pots are clanking, but a deep smile faces me from behind the stainless-steel shelving where the dishes are put.

"Well, looky here!" my cousin Linus shouts, wiping his hands on a dish towel and rounding the crowded area to come over to me. He lifts his hands in case I struggle to hear him with everything going on back here. *Not like you to use the Bailey name.*

I giggle and shrug.

I'm not sure what to say. My date didn't realize that even restaurants in small towns get busy?

I step out from our two-person circle and put my arm out toward Matt, continuing to sign since it's so loud in here. *Matt, this is my cousin, Linus. Linus, this is Matt—*

Peterson. Linus signs, putting out his hand. *Are you telling me your name didn't work with Cami?* Linus speaks as well as signs.

Matt chuckles, his easygoing personality shining through. *Nope. Palmer got us in. And the chef's table at that?* He looks at me with eyes filled with admiration. A look most women would die to have facing them, but I feel nothing stirring inside. *Impressive.*

Shit, he can sign? Linus grins. *He must be a keeper.*

I have no idea what to say, other than I don't think he is. At least not for me. Linus walks behind my back, over to the small table for two where we can still see them working but the noise level is a few decibels lower.

I hope to impress you. Have a seat and enjoy. Do you have any allergies, Matt? Linus smiles at me because he knows I don't have any.

Linus is in my age bracket in the Bailey clan and was

one of my biggest confidants during our high school years. When he decided to follow in his dad's footsteps and become a chef, he was adamant about doing it on his own terms. After returning from his training all over the world, he concentrated on Asian cuisine while Uncle Rome is all about European. Linus and my other cousin, Lance, are partners in this new restaurant in the resort, The Bamboo Spoon.

None. Matt sighs.

Great, let me go prepare some specialities. Linus runs his hand over the back of my shoulders as he walks back to the kitchen.

I really want to tug Linus down and get his advice about these feelings for Hudson that are suddenly rising inside me. Why, when I have this hot guy next to me, is all I can think of a man who has been in my life for years.

Thoughts of the past rush through my head as the waitress comes by and pours us some wine that Linus apparently suggested. Memories of when I first met Hudson and how I didn't want the drama of his baggage. Because baggage only leads to heartbreak. There was a short time I thought maybe I was wrong to place him in the friend category. Back then, he practically was a boyfriend to me, picking me up from work, cooking dinners, even taking care of me when I was sick.

Then I got pregnant with Adley, and I just couldn't cross that line. I wanted Adley to have two parents in her life, and fear stopped me from allowing myself to fully feel for Hudson.

A warm hand touches my arm, and my mind returns to Matt and the restaurant. What is wrong with me?

"Sorry," I say, feeling my cheeks heat.

Matt smiles, one that all the girls probably fall head over heels for. "I lost you for a minute."

I shake my head. "Sorry, I'm just in the middle of this book that I'm writing, and I think it's consuming my thoughts a little too much."

Yes, that must be the reason all this stuff with Hudson is surfacing. It's the story. It has to be.

"It amazes me that you're a writer. How do you come up with all your ideas?" He picks up his wineglass and leans back in his chair, waiting for me to answer.

Matt doesn't seem like a wine guy. He seems like a beer and shots guy. Maybe it's the snowboarder thing, and how back in the day, I spent most of my time with snowboarders. For those eight months, Hudson's snowboarding friends practically lived with us. And all they did was drink beer, do shots, and eat Chinese food.

"It used to come easier. This book was really hard to start, but now that I'm on a roll, I can't type fast enough." I refrain from telling him that I kind of wish I was with my laptop right now.

"That's great," he says before sipping his wine.

I take a sip of the wine, loving that Linus picked a white he knew I'd love. "And you? How did you become a snowboarder?"

He talks for the next twenty minutes about his snowboarding career, starting from the first time his dad put him on a board. We go through appetizers and soup before he's finished telling me all about from childhood up until the last trick he did this afternoon on the halfpipe.

I smile politely, eating the delicious food Linus has made, drinking my wine, but somewhere along the line, I tune out. The next part of my story plays in my head like a movie.

Bea and Pete stumbled into their apartment door. She fiddled in her purse, searching for her keys while Pete laughed. Bea ended up dumping the contents of her purse all over the dirty floor in the hallway of her apartment building, and the keys jingled as they fell to the floor.

Pete picked them up and dangled them in front of her face. "You're drunk!"

Bea swiped them away from him and inserted her key into the door. "So are you!"

She walked in and Pete bent down to pick up her lipstick, wallet, and phone from among the receipts and change scattered on the floor.

"You left all your shit!" he shouted too loudly while Bea watched him, holding the door open.

She just laughed until Mr. Overfelt opened his door and scowled at them. Their laughter died quickly.

"Sorry, Mr. Overfelt," Bea said.

He stared long and hard, then shut his door and flipped the lock.

"Come on," Bea whispered, or at least she tried unsuccessfully to keep her voice down.

Pete walked into the apartment, taking the door from her and shutting it, placing his finger over his mouth. "Shh…"

Their faces were so close together, and they both had their fingers over their mouths, telling one another to be quiet. Their eyes locked, and for the first time, neither of them turned away.

The longer they stared into each other's eyes, the more something changed between them. Like a hunk of clay, it changed shape and meaning. They didn't laugh again, and Pete leaned forward, the finger that was over his lips now shifting to touch her face.

Bea stepped back, her eyes darting away. "I need water."

She was just steps away from the kitchen when Pete

grabbed her hand and tugged her back into his arms. Bea had no time to prepare herself. When Pete's lips met hers, she froze. Having no idea what to do, she stood there, but Pete wouldn't accept it.

She hadn't moved from his embrace. She didn't step back or push him off. So he continued to press his lips to hers, and his hand went to the back of her head. He swiped his tongue along the seam of her lips, and she succumbed, opening for him.

Her hands went up and wound around his neck, pulling him closer. Neither said a word, their lips and hands doing all the talking. Pete couldn't get enough of her, couldn't get close enough. Her body pressed against his felt too damn good.

They somehow managed to make it into the bedroom, falling into her dresser.

"Fuck," Pete said, knowing he'd have a bruise by morning.

Bea giggled, and Pete grabbed her ass with both hands and picked her up so her legs wound around his waist. They circled and kissed, lost in a whirlwind of lust. Slamming against the wall, Pete tried to draw back slightly to take off Bea's shirt, but their equilibrium was off since they were drunk, and he went too far back, causing Bea to grab at the curtains, tearing them down as she tried not to fall.

Both of them lay in a fit of giggles for a moment before they disregarded what had happened, came together again, their lips unable to part except when undressing the other. They fell onto the bed, Bea on top of Pete, and all the laughter stopped as he entered her fast and hard from below.

Their eyes got lost in one another as he withdrew and slid back in, circling his hips. back arched, wanting more...

A touch on my shoulder makes me realize I'm lost in my thoughts again. Shit. I look up to see Matt staring over my shoulder. The smile he's worn the entire night isn't there, and it's been replaced with what almost looks like a scowl.

When I glance to my right, a figure comes out from behind me. Hudson bends down, and I turn in his direction. He takes my hands for a moment and squeezes them before letting go to sign, *we need to talk.*

PALMER

I blink to make sure I'm not seeing things, but it wouldn't be the first time he's rescued me when I didn't realize I needed saving. Did Hudson somehow realize that I should be writing my book and not be on a date?

"What are you doing here?" I ask.

"I have the same question," Matt chimes in, and Hudson and I turn in his direction.

"Is it Adley? Is everything okay?" I ignore Matt, but I'm pretty sure if it was her, Hudson would've called and not just shown up.

He looks at Matt. "I'm sorry." Then he bends down again and takes my hands. "This might sound crazy, and if I'm in this alone, then so be it, but Palmer..."

I swallow past the dryness in my throat. Why does this feel like a proposal or something? But that's ridiculous. Neither of us believes you need a marriage license to spend your life with someone.

I stare at him, because I should be able to see the intention in his eyes. He's always been transparent to me, but right now, I'm confused.

"And here's the entrée…oh shit." Linus stands next to the table with another server holding out two plates. Linus's eyebrows raise when he sees Hudson crouched down next to me.

"Well, at least I'm getting a good meal," Matt says as the server places his dish in front of him.

She does the same for me, and Linus stands there frozen, apparently not sure what to do.

Hell, I don't know what to do.

Matt picks up his fork and digs into his meal.

"Lately, these feelings…" Hudson trails off again. He's got that nervousness he gets when he's trying to be open with me. Like a shelter dog who looks like he wants you to pet him but can't trust you yet. Maybe he needs to hear that.

"What is it? It's me." I squeeze his hand.

He nods a few times as if he's silently convincing himself to speak whatever it is he came here for. "I don't want you on a date with Matt. I don't want you to sleep with him."

"Mission accomplished," Matt grumbles over his mouthful of food.

"I don't want to sleep with Matt either," I confess.

"Great. What a perfect date," Matt says, sarcasm loaded in his words.

"What about Theresa?"

Hudson shakes his head. "We broke up."

My shoulders sink. "I'm sorry." I wasn't always her biggest fan, but he seemed to really like her for a while.

A smile tips his lips. "You're not understanding…we broke up because I want you."

The air whooshes from my lungs. My heart flips, and my stomach feels as if a million little tumblers are inside. "Oh."

"You could've told me, man," Matt interrupts.

I want to put up my hand and shush Matt. But I'm still processing the fact that my best friend sees me more as than a friend and might be having some of the same feelings I've had lately.

Hudson turns to Matt. "I'm sorry, man. I never thought...I mean..."

"Yeah, I suspected I should've just stayed away. I knew it on the hill the other day." He shoves another forkful of food into his mouth.

"I was still figuring it out."

He chuckles and leans back, swallowing his food. "It's all good, man. I'd never would've stepped in if you'd said anything." He wipes his mouth with the napkin, picks up his wineglass and downs the rest, then stands. "I'm gonna head out. You two...well..." He looks at both of us. "Good luck."

He shakes Linus's hand and thanks him for an incredible meal, telling him that he'll be back for another meal before he leaves town. The two of them continue to talk and walk out, leaving Hudson and me alone.

The room closes in, and I can barely breathe now that this impromptu surprise is sinking in. I stand, and Hudson follows suit.

"Palmer?" he asks, looking worried.

I put up my hand, keeping my back to him. This is a huge step. A step that could fuck up everything we've built.

"What's the matter? You don't feel the same way?" I hear him coming closer to me.

I shake my head, turning to face him. "That's not it. I've

been feeling something too. But if we...we could...you know...mess it all up. And Adley."

He takes my hands. "Adley has two parents who love each other. Two parents who have been in denial about their feelings for one another. Two parents who could raise her under one roof with both of us there when she wakes in the morning and to tuck her in at night."

Hope surfaces in his blue eyes. It all sounds so nice. Like a fairy tale, but fairy tales are just that, stories someone wrote. I know that better than anyone.

"And if we sleep together and then all this"—I motion between us—"just evaporates? What then for our daughter?"

"Is that what you think?" He drops my hands. "That I'm saying all this because I want to have sex with you? Jesus, Palmer." He turns away from me.

I close my eyes, step forward, and place my hands on his back.

"It's never been about sex with you. I fucking love you, Palmer."

He says the last part so softly that I place my cheek lightly on his back, closing my eyes as if it's going to let me process this abrupt change in our relationship. His back rises and falls with his breaths, and I relish the smell of him. A smell that's always felt like home to me.

I owe him my honesty.

"I'm scared for her," I admit. It's easier to say with his back to me. "I don't want to fuck her up."

He turns around, circling his arms around me, and I wrap my arms around his waist. "She's my number one priority. You know that, right?"

I nod, because we both agree on one thing—Adley comes first, always.

"But I don't want to deny myself anymore. I want you, Palmer, and if you want me too, then I want us to give this a try. If you want to keep it from Adley until we have some more time to discover what could be, that's fine, but I'm not going to just take a back seat like I did all those years ago." He places his finger under my chin and eases my face up to look at him. "I know you're scared, but you've always been able to trust me, right?"

I nod.

"Then trust me and jump into this with me. Let us explore this without any walls up."

I lose myself in the depth of the love pouring out of his eyes. "I..."

He lowers his head to mine, his lips so close, his breath tickles my nostrils.

"Trust me," he whispers.

I nod. "Okay." I inch a little closer, but he draws back.

"Say you love me."

"Hudson," I sigh, and he chuckles, inching back when I rise on my tiptoes to reach him. He's not going to let this go. I feel as if there's nowhere left to hide anyway, so I speak the truth. "I love you. I always have."

His finger moves, and he cradles my face, tilting it up to look at him. "You're gonna love me so much more now."

I shake my head. "There's that ego."

"You love my ego." He lowers his head to mine, the tips of our noses touching. "I'm going to kiss you now."

I slide my tongue out to lick my lips. "Okay."

He tilts his head, and he places a feather-light kiss on my lips. My eyes close, and those tumblers jump around in my stomach again.

The kiss doesn't stay sweet and tentative for long. My hands slide behind his neck and his fall to my waist, tugging me flush against him. Our lips press more firmly to one another and I'm not sure whose tongue seeks entrance first, but they glide against each other and the sultriest moan rumbles inside me.

God, he's such a good kisser. That's one thing that's never left my memory.

His hands run up and down my back, pushing me into him as if he can't get me close enough. I'm not objecting. I want to climb him, Velcro myself to him, so we're never not touching.

He strips his lips from mine, and his lips travel to my ear. "Is Harper staying the night?"

"She wasn't planning on it." My fingers run through his sandy-blond hair, loving the sweet kisses he's giving me under my ear.

"Can she?"

"We can call and ask."

He pulls away, and I reach for him. "Call her."

"We can go home. Adley will be asleep."

He shakes his head. "Ask her."

I hate to admit it, but I like this bossy side. I walk over to my chair, immediately aware that we've been making out in the middle of a restaurant kitchen, and pull out my phone.

> Can you spend the night? I can be home early in the morning.

I send the text, not sure what Hudson is thinking. If we go to his house, Harper will probably see us.

> Finally getting some? Done. Now stop texting me.

Thanks.

She probably assumes it's Matt, and I'm not going to correct her.

Put the phone down. Have fun. Break some stuff. I'll be expecting details tomorrow.

Hudson stands back, his hands in his pockets, waiting for my answer. I nod and put my phone back in my purse. He grabs my hand, winding us through the kitchen.

"See you two," Linus says, and I barely see the smile on his face before we're through the restaurant.

Hudson is on a mission, but he stops me outside the lobby's ladies' room. "Go inside and I'll text you."

"What?" I shake my head.

"Trust me?"

"Well, yeah, but..."

He opens the door for me. An elderly woman scowls as she's walking out, and Hudson is quick to apologize. His expression says for me to follow the directions he's giving, so I let the door close.

While I'm here, I might as well look at myself and make sure my makeup is all right. Ten minutes later, I'm pacing the length of the restroom and becoming worried, but my phone finally dings with a text.

Room 434

My back falls against the wall, and I put my hand over my heart. He got us a hotel room?

My phone lights up with another text.

Watch out for eyes.

God, he is smart, because if we got ratted out in Buzz Wheel, that would be the worst. Especially after I was on a date with someone else, and he just broke up with Theresa. Linus knows enough not to say anything. We made a pact years ago not to give away each other's gossip to that stupid app. I can only hope that everyone in the kitchen was too busy working to notice Hudson and me kissing.

I slide out of the bathroom and look both ways. There are a few people lingering in the lobby, but I don't recognize them, so I head out, trying to think of how to avoid being recognized as I make my way to the bank of elevators. Then I realize if I really want to be careful, there's only one way.

Turning back around, I head down the hall to the stairway. I walk up the four flights of stairs, open the door to the hallway, and peek out. It's empty, so I push the door all the way open and rush down the hall to door 434.

Nerves rack my body as I raise my fist to knock on the door and pause.

You can do this. It's Hudson.

I'm about to knock when the door swings open.

Our eyes lock and a warm smile bursts across Hudson's face. "What are you waiting for?"

"You." I step in, and the door closes behind me.

nineteen

PALMER

I step into the plush hotel room my uncle remodeled years ago when he bought the hotel and turned it into the go-to resort in Alaska.

The king-sized bed is a beacon for what's going to happen here, wrapped in a big white comforter with fluffy pillows. A comforter we'll share, that we'll lie naked under. The last time we had sex, we were drunk and didn't care where we were getting it on.

Look how far we've come. He paid an ungodly amount for a room when we each have a house less than ten minutes away. That, and we're both stone-cold sober and very aware of what we're doing. Knowing the chances we're taking, the repercussions.

My anxiety ramps up and panic rises inside me.

Hudson wraps his arms around my waist, nuzzling his head into my neck. "Relax. You should know I don't have any condoms on me. I didn't come here thinking about what might happen after my spiel. But I always used a condom with Theresa."

"I'm on the pill, you know that." After Adley was born, I went on it right away.

"There's no pressure from me. We can do other stuff." His hand traces a path down my arm, and I repress a shiver.

"I want to feel you inside me, Hudson. We don't need a condom."

I feel his body relax behind mine. "Can I take your implants out?"

I nod.

He draws back and reaches along my ear, removing my right cochlear implant. His touch is soft and gentle, just as he's always been with me. I want to thank him for understanding me so deeply. He's leading me to where we both want to go slowly because he knows I'm not as comfortable as he is with affection.

After he takes off my right cochlear implant, he takes off my left, and I close my eyes at the silence. He must put them on the dresser, but his hands are back around my waist and his face returns to my neck, placing soft and sweet kisses there. Then he slides my hair over my shoulder, his lips exploring the back of my neck.

My eyelids flutter, but I keep them open, my hands reaching back to his thighs, wanting to feel the connection to him.

He feels so good, I want to turn around. I want to kiss him, touch his face, and look into his eyes, but I don't want him to stop this exploration of my body. The only other time we were together, it was fast and crazy. Yeah, it was the hottest sex I've ever had, but this time, I want to enjoy him taking his time.

Shifting his attention to the other side of my neck, he moves my hair again, and I arch my neck, allowing him full access. A cool breeze flows along the side of my body from him unzipping my dress. With a feather-light touch, he lowers the strap of my dress and I help by sliding out my arm. We repeat the same on the other side and the fabric drops, exposing my bra-covered breasts.

His hands find my hips, and he turns me around, his eyes meeting mine before dropping down to see my barely covered breasts. I've never allowed a man to stare unapologetically at my body. My self-confidence isn't as high as it could be since I'm not exactly thin. And the last time Hudson saw me like this, although I doubt he remembers, my stomach didn't bear the light stretch marks they do now.

My self-consciousness wins, and I cross my arms over my stomach.

His head tilts, and he shakes his head, then pries my arms away. His thumbs run across the length of the stretch marks, and he smiles. My breath hitches as I watch him, feeling his intimate touch over the marks that are proof of me bearing our daughter. Tears prick my eyes.

Hudson continues, his hands falling down, sinking under the waist of my dress, pushing the fabric down over my hips. It pools on the floor, and he falls to his knees, placing his lips on the stretch marks.

He draws back and signs the word beautiful.

I want to shake my head and tell him he's crazy, but I don't. My hands run through the silky strands at the back of his head while his lips travel a path up my torso, until he's standing over me again.

He's way too overdressed, so I reach for the hem of his shirt and slide my hands underneath, feeling the smoothness of his stomach, the grooves of his abs. His T-shirt rises with my movement, and he reaches back to the neckline and pulls it up and over his head.

He's so hot—why am I just enjoying this now? Especially since Hudson is so much more than just a hot male.

He runs his fingers down my arm until my hand is secure in his. When he leads me over to the bed, I sit on the edge, and my fingers go to the button on his jeans. I pull down his pants and his boxer briefs while he caresses my shoulders and neck. Once he's naked in front of me, his cock springs up. He's gifted in that department too. Because I was drunk the night we were together, I barely remember the feeling of him inside me. I just remember thinking how good it felt.

I inch forward, but he holds me back with his hands on my shoulder. I look up and he shakes his head, smirking. He eases me down until my back hits the soft mattress, and he hooks his fingers into the sides of my thong, pulling it down my legs and disposing of it on the floor.

I scoot up on the bed to give us more room, and he places one knee down and leans down, getting on his stomach. His hands glide up the inside of my thighs, and he again casts teasing kisses along my sensitive flesh until he reaches my core.

The stroke of his tongue surprises me, and my back rises off the mattress. He picks up his head, a playful smile on his lips before he disappears between my legs again. He laps at me with deep and dragging licks. My skin burns, and my body craves more. He gives it to me without me having to ask, his mouth closing over my clit, sucking it into his hot, wet mouth. I tug at his hair, my back flying off the mattress.

His arms slide under my legs, pulling me harder against his face while he continues to manipulate my body, giving me the pleasure I seek until my orgasm crashes down, and my eyes roll back in my head. He allows me to ride out the orgasm, but I need more. I need him inside me as I look into his eyes.

Being deaf, sex can be hard at times. I can't hear the noises my partner makes. The small grunts and moans and growls from enjoying an act that takes you to the brink of losing control. There's no dirty talk unless I'm on top and still have my implants on, so I have to go off feel and look. So I want to stare into his eyes and watch him come.

I tug on his hair, and he slides up my body until the tip of him runs through my wetness. I offer my hips, and he slides inside me, sinking deeper with each thrust. He holds his weight off me with his elbows on either side of me, and his lips meet mine.

We kiss in a tangled web of pleasure while our hearts pound against one another's chests. It feels as if we're addicted to touching each other's skin because both our hands keep roaming over the other's body.

He pulls back a bit and stares at me, circling his hips, grinding his pelvis along my clit. Sex with Hudson is like entering another dimension. It's so intense I can barely hang on, clenching down to try to stop myself from combusting.

I watch as his eyes darken with desire, and his hips move faster and harder. He's there, and I am too. Pulling his head down, I kiss him, hoping every ounce of what I feel for him is conveyed through my actions, that he feels the energy in this room too.

It all becomes too much, and I can't hold back anymore. My orgasm rolls through me, my insides gripping him tightly, my body arching from the bed until every muscle contracts. Hudson pulls back, watching me as bliss floats through me and my back slowly sinks back down, my body becomes tranquil and calm.

He pounds into me with raw, rapid thrusts until his torso rises up from mine, and his neck pulls back, his eyes rolling back. He pumps into me a few times before he stills, and his eyes shut for only a moment. When they open and our eyes meet, there's only love exchanged between us.

I push back the tears that well up because I've never been handled like this, never experienced such emotion when having sex. And the fact it's with Hudson only makes it better.

He remains on top of me, unmoving for a moment. I'm not complaining. I don't want to part either. But eventually he slides out of me and heads into the bathroom.

I panic for a moment, knowing that what just happened changes everything. My fight-or-flight instinct is riding me hard—my mind begging me to grab my clothes and run. That voice at the back of my head tells me it was hormones, not love that brought us into this room. Now that it's out of our system, we'll go back to co-parenting our daughter as we always have.

Hudson emerges with a washcloth in hand and cleans me up before disappearing into the bathroom again. When he returns, he crawls in next to me and wraps his arms around my body. I go to him, like an addict to their drug of choice. All that panic and doubt ripples away in the safety of his arms.

We might be headed toward trouble, but I don't care right now. No one has to know what we're doing. It can be our little secret. What's the harm in that?

HUDSON

Palmer's long dark hair spills across the white pillowcase as she sleeps peacefully next to me.

I've been sitting here for over an hour, watching her back rise and fall. Fear that she would be gone rippled through me when I first woke this morning. Palmer has reservations about love, about trust, about letting people in. She's been honest with me about the turmoil she went through when she was fourteen and found out about her parents' past.

Her dad started drinking too much around the time of her mom's pregnancy with her, causing her to eventually leave him. He didn't arrive back in Palmer's life until she was eighteen months old. She grew up thinking she had the perfect family, the perfect father—until she googled him when she was fourteen.

I'm not sure if she felt lied to all those years, and that's where her trust issues come from, or if it's hurt that her dad wasn't there for the first part of her life, but she rarely wants to talk about it, and I never force the issue. But now, I think we need to. If we're going to give this thing between us an honest try, she's got to work through it.

And as if we don't have enough to figure out, Buzz Wheel reported on me this morning.

When I first moved to Lake Starlight, I thought the whole gossip app thing was small-town fun—until I found myself in it. More than once. I get that Buzz Wheel started years ago, and being that the Baileys are like the damn Kennedys in Lake Starlight, everyone seems to be obsessed with what's going on in their lives. Maybe it's because Palmer's grandparents died young, and her uncle Austin agreed to take over the care of his siblings while her aunt Savannah took over the family company, Bailey Timber, which employs a lot of people in the area.

I read through the post on the app once again, wondering how much trouble it'll cause for us.

We're starting today off with a BANG! But there's a bit of mystery in what I'm about to tell you. Turns out that Hudson Fisher arrived at Glacier Point last night and rented a room. Why would a resident who owns a perfectly good house close to downtown rent a room at the luxurious and expensive resort? That's the question we're asking too. From what witnesses have said, he was by himself and had no luggage or bags with him. Seems suspicious if you ask me. We all know he was entertaining SOMEONE, but the question is WHO?

For those of you new to Lake Starlight, Hudson shares a daughter with Palmer Ferguson, daughter of Sedona (nee Bailey) and Jamison Ferguson. They raise their daughter together as best friends. I think I can say for all of us that whoever he's entertaining, he's being secretive, which means he doesn't want us to know who it is. But that just makes us want to know even more. Anyone with any details, you know what to do. You'll know when I know!

In other news, someone saw Kenzie Whitmore buying a pregnancy test. We might just have another Bailey on the way. Brooklyn Whitmore (nee Bailey) has a pep in her step lately. Maybe she knows something the rest of us don't!

I don't bother reading the rest and toss my phone on the nightstand.

Palmer rolls over, and her eyes flutter open. She stretches like a cat, her back arching, her arms over her head. It's adorable. Her eyes open fully, and a timid smile creases her lips.

"Good morning," I say, knowing she can read my lips.

She nuzzles into my body and wraps her arms around my waist.

We lie together under the comfy comforter, but I know we have to bite the bullet eventually.

After I made love to her last night, we took a shower and ended up having sex again. Then I woke her up once more in the middle of the night when I rolled toward her and felt her soft skin under my palms. There was no resisting, no matter how tired either of us were. It's like now that I can have her, I can't possibly get enough.

I slide out from under her, and she sits up against the headboard, a look of surprise on her face. Grabbing her cochlear implants, I bring them over to her, and she goes to grab them, but I circle my finger, telling her to turn her back to me. Then I put them on for her.

She fiddles with them when I'm done. "What's going on, Hudson?"

I pick up my phone off the nightstand and hand it to her.

She looks at me, biting the inside of her cheek as she does when she's worried. "What?"

"Just read it."

She looks down and sighs. "Buzz Wheel?" Her face falls, but when she gets to the point that her cousin, Lance's wife, might be pregnant, she smiles. "They don't know it's me." She hands me back my phone.

"Palmer, they're gonna know."

She shakes her head. "Linus won't tell anyone. You can tell Matt to keep it to himself."

"And the kitchen staff? All the people in the restaurant? I had your hand in mine."

She goes over to the chair that has our clothes lying over the back. Great, she's going to flee now and probably dodge me for the rest of the day. But to my surprise, she takes my shirt and slips it on. The hem hits her mid-thigh, and a caveman's possessiveness comes alive inside me at seeing her in my clothes.

"We're friends. You hold my hand a lot. And no one heard our conversation. If anything, people might think that you were consoling me after Matt left."

I guess I'm glad she's not freaking out, but still, a layer of disappointment settles inside me since she doesn't say, "Who cares if anyone knows about us?" I'm not sure why I would assume she'd wake up and want to shout our newfound relationship from the window of the resort. I told her we could keep it a secret, and I can't change the game now. But last night was so...not what I expected. I thought it would be like last time when we ripped off each other's clothes and bumped into walls and furniture before we found our way to the bed.

Something came over me when I saw her fear as she stared at the bed, and I wanted to ease that hesitancy inside her. I wanted her to know how much I care for her, how much I love her, and how much I see a future for us. Regardless, I told her we'd take it slow, and if that's what she needs, then I'll do it.

"Anyone could have seen us. It's Lake Starlight."

She nods and saunters over to the bed, puts one knee on the mattress, and swings her leg over my lap, straddling me. "We have about three hours before checkout. Do you want to spend the whole time talking about Buzz Wheel?"

"I thought you'd be more worried," I say, my hands landing on her hips.

She grinds down against my length, already wet and ready. "I told you. No one knows anything. Trust me." She uses my words against me. "So, are we done talking?"

I roll her over and hover over her. "Yes."

She rolls me back, lifting and just barely sliding me inside her. "I want to hear you," she says because we both know she can't keep her cochlear implants on if she's on her back. There's too much risk of damaging them.

She sinks down on me, and damn, she feels so damn good. My hands find her hips once more, and her hands land on my shoulders.

"Let's get this off you." I grab the hem of the T-shirt and pull it up her torso.

She lifts her hands away from my shoulders so I can get it off. Her tits are in my face, so my hands slide up the sides of her abdomen before I take each one in hand. She rocks back, placing her palms on my thighs, offering herself to me as she shifts her weight up and down. Each thrust is more painfully exquisite than the one before it.

"Fuck, Palmer," I pant, pumping my hips to reach the depths of her pussy. She's so wet, so slick, I try to think of anything but coming.

"I know," she says. "You're a perfect fit."

I want to tell her I am a perfect fit, her only fit, and the last man that she'll ever have. That would be wrong, though, because I don't know if I'm ruining every other man after me for her, but she sure as shit is ruining every woman for me from this day forward. Not that it matters. I only want her.

"These tits."

She shifts her weight forward, her hands landing on the top of the headboard as I take a nipple into my mouth. Sucking, licking, nibbling. The sounds she makes...the moans, the sharp intakes of breath...I get why she wanted to hear me this morning.

"Oh, Jesus." Her back arches back, and my mouth falls off her tit. She circles her hips. "Don't move. I'm so close."

She picks up the pace, and I grab her hips to help her get there faster. I'm practically picking her up and pulling her down onto my dick. Curse words fall from her perfect lips, and I pull her mouth down on mine, stilling inside her the moment our tongues meet.

Her body tenses, and we come at the same time, our moans making the perfect symphony. We continue to kiss as I grow soft inside her, her tits pressing against my sweaty chest.

"I could watch you come for a lifetime," I say, and she inches back, our eyes meeting.

"Me too."

We draw closer again, our lips meeting in a languid kiss that conveys the feelings we admitted last night.

When we close the kiss, she sits up, slowly moving off me. "We really are stupid that it took us this long." She slides off the mattress and walks naked into the bathroom, and my eyes follow her. She returns with a washcloth. "My turn to clean you up."

She runs the washcloth over my dick, and her touch springs life back into it.

"Are you ever satisfied?" she jokes and disappears back into the bathroom. This time, she shuts the door. Seconds later, the toilet flushes and water runs from the faucet. When she returns, she grabs her clothes from the chair. "Do you mind taking Adley today? I'm getting to the good part of my book."

I sit on the bed, my back against the headboard, watching her intently. "Palmer, what are you doing?"

She zips up her dress and walks over to me. "It's not like that. I'm not running. I just have to finish this book, but how about a family movie night?"

We haven't had many of those lately—really, not since Theresa came into my life. Usually when Palmer had Adley, I'd spend my time at her place with them, but when I had Adley, Palmer either worked or Theresa would be over.

I place my hands on Palmer's cheeks and stare into her eyes, trying to see the fight-or-flight in her blue eyes. But it's not there, so I believe she's not running away from me. "Okay. Make your own pizza night?"

She kisses me quickly. "Can't wait."

She sits on the side of the bed, pulling out her phone, and I hover, seeing her texting Harper to come get her.

"She thinks you spent the night with Matt. She might put two and two together after she sees Buzz Wheel."

She swivels around to face me. "No, because if anyone asks why you spent the night here, you're going to tell them that you were just getting some space."

"I'm not sure anyone—"

She puts her finger over my lips. "They will. Now, get ready so after I get home, you can return and get Adley. I'll text you when I'm done writing."

"I don't get it. Where are you going to write?"

She smiles, her secret one, the one she puts on when she's not going to tell me. "Maybe one day you'll find out. But right now, I'm not telling anyone. I have to finish this book."

She grabs her purse and kisses me goodbye, but when she tries to stop, my hand runs along her neck, and I pull her back down to me. I kiss her thoroughly, pouring all my emotions in just so she remembers me when she walks out that door.

She laughs and shakes her head, fully aware of what I'm doing.

"You want me to trust you, so trust me, okay?" She walks across the hotel room, opens the door, blows me a kiss, and walks out.

I miss her already.

twenty-one

PALMER

It takes all my willpower to leave the hotel room with Hudson still there and even more when I get in the car with Harper not to tell her everything. Good thing Adley is in the back seat.

"Mommy!" she says in a tired voice.

I turn to sign to her while I speak outloud. *Hey, sweetie. Did you have fun with Harper?*

With a sleepy smile, she raises her hands to show me her painted nails. "Look."

Very pretty.

"Buckle up," Harper says to me.

I put on my seat belt, and she accelerates a little too fast for my liking. Especially with my daughter in the back.

"So?" She looks in the rearview mirror at Adley.

I shrug. "So nothing."

"Don't you dare hide details. I told you—"

"Harp, there's a three-year-old in the back."

"She's already half asleep. We stayed up a little past her bedtime last night."

"How late?" I frown.

The sheepish grin on her face tells me all I need to know. "I'm not going to stop asking. You sleep with one of the hottest guys in snowboarding, and you're not going to tell me about it? Although Dax Campbell is more my type."

I shake my head at her love of snowboarders. "He's married to that other medalist, Demi Harrison, isn't he?"

"Oh, I can do what she did." Harper waves it off.

"You're a wedding planner, not a skier," I inform her in case she forgot how different her job is than going seventy miles per hour downhill.

"Dealing with bridezillas is ten times harder and more dangerous, just in a different way. She might fall and die, and I might get shanked."

Laugher spills out of me. "They have kids."

"Ask Adley, I'd make an excellent stepmom." She stops at a light and smiles at me.

"You have an excuse for everything." I glance back and see Adley's cheek resting along the one side of the car seat. She's out.

"Hey." Harper smacks my leg to grab my attention.

"You don't have to hit me."

"Did you read Buzz Wheel?" She ignores my comment.

I nibble my cheek and look out the window. "No." I hate lying. She presses on the gas when the light turns green, and I fly back into the seat. "Jeez, Harp."

"Hudson was there last night too."

Okay, I can either be straight or continue to lie through my teeth.

"I have to tell you something," I relent—mostly because what happened last night is a lot, and I need to download. And Harper, although she loves gossip, has never outed any of my secrets. She knew I was pregnant before I arrived in Lake Starlight and told no one.

"That Hudson came into the restaurant and confessed his undying love for you, then he got a hotel room, and the two of you had wild sex all night?" She smiles smugly for a moment before returning her attention to the road.

I look over my shoulder to make sure Adley is still asleep. "How did you know that?"

"I have eyes everywhere in this town."

"Are you Buzz Wheel?"

She laughs and hits the steering wheel with her hand. "Hell no...let's just say there was a chatty chef texting me last night."

Jeez, Linus. I thought I could trust him.

She pats my knee and squeezes. "Your secret is safe with me. But why are you being secretive about it? I mean, the two of you have a daughter." She looks in the rearview mirror.

"I don't know. I'm kind of confused."

"What?" She stops the car in the middle of the road and stares at me, lowering her voice. "You slept with him without knowing if you had feelings? I hate to break it to you, but bad decision. You two have such a great thing going, and that kinda thing is gonna blow it up."

"I never said I didn't have feelings. I just have to make sure this is going to work before we tell Adley."

She puts her hand over her heart. "Thank God, because that man loves you something fierce, and if you break his heart just because you're scared—"

"Why does everyone think I'm scared or I'm gonna run? It's starting to piss me off." In truth, it's only been her and Hudson, but they're two of the people who know me the best.

"Everyone knows you harbor some things because of your parents' past."

I roll my eyes. "I handled that. Sure, it messed with me when I was younger, but you know I don't like baggage, which is why I let mine go a long time ago."

She sighs and moves the car forward again. She's holding something back.

"What, Harp? Just say it."

"Nothing. I'm happy for you two, and I won't tell anyone. You know me, you, and Linus keep our secrets between us."

I nod, but her reaction to my words triggers me to find out exactly what she means.

"Please tell me," I say as she pulls into my driveway.

She turns off the ignition and faces me. "I hate to break it to you, but everyone has baggage. Your issue with your parents is your baggage, and Hudson might have more baggage than you know." I open my mouth, and she raises her hand. "Everyone comes with baggage, Palm. Even you. That's life."

I open my door and place one foot on the driveway. "I have to go write. Hudson is going to be here shortly to get Adley. Do you mind staying just a little longer?"

She gives me her expression like what the hell is wrong with you, we're in the middle of a conversation. Then her shoulders sink, and she nods. "Of course. All I have to do today is get with Maven about a bride's flowers that are on backorder."

"Thank you. I owe you big."

"A dedication would be nice." She smiles.

I hope she understands I heard her, but if I think too hard about what she's saying, I might freak out and run, and I can't do that to Hudson. I don't *want* to do it to Hudson.

"Done." I lean forward and kiss her cheek.

I hate leaving Adley after an entire night away from her, but if I don't finish this book, I can't feed my little girl. I go inside and change quickly before grabbing my bag and heading to the cabin.

A SENSE of peace envelops me when I enter the cabin, though my mind is on Hudson. I get myself situated, open my laptop, and read the chapter I wrote about Bea and Pete and the morning after.

The morning after they slept together, Pete went into the kitchen and made pancakes. He didn't know how Bea was going to react, and he worried that he'd be looking for a new best friend and a new apartment.

He was just finishing the first batch when she walked in, her hair a mess but her cochlear implants in place. He smiled to himself. Last night was one of the best of his life, even if it was a little fuzzy. They had slept together, and it was just as he imagined it would be. Combustive. Explosive.

"Good morning," he said.

She grabbed the pot of coffee he'd brewed and poured a cup. "Mornin'." She brought the cup to her lips and sipped. "Tell me you're just as hungover as I am."

"I chugged two glasses of water and took some pain meds. Yours are on the table."

She walked over and stared at the pills and the water. She didn't put down her coffee mug or take the pills or the water. She just stared, her eyes glued to the two white pills.

Pete brought over the first plate of pancakes and set them in front of her. A lone tear fell from her eye and onto the table.

He grabbed her shoulders, turning her to face him. "Bea, what is it?"

Her head slowly rose, and Pete saw it there. The hope that had sprung inside him after last night plummeted as quickly as a fall from the halfpipe. One misstep and boom, game over. But he didn't think they'd made a misstep. He'd thought things might finally be moving forward with Bea.

"What's wrong?"

"I don't want to lose you." She stepped into Pete and wrapped her arms around his waist so tightly he felt his lungs struggle to breathe.

He held her for a few minutes before asking, "What are you talking about?"

She stepped back and wiped the tears that were flowing down her cheeks. "Because we slept together, and now you're making me pancakes and leaving me pain meds and water. You want a relationship, and I'm not sure I can go there."

Pete laughed then registered the smell of smoke from the pancakes on the stove. He ran over and turned off the burner, tossing the pan to the other side of the stove.

"Now I ruined the pancakes," Bea wailed.

Pete laughed. "What the hell is going on? I would have done this had I slept on the couch all night." He was being truthful, but at the same time, he was pushing down the hope that maybe Bea would be ready for a relationship with him. He'd played the friend card for a year, and they'd gotten to know each other better than anyone else in their lives.

She shrugged. "You mean you don't expect a relationship now that we slept together?"

"Bea, it's pancakes, water, and pain meds. I didn't order six dozen roses and heart-shaped candy and teddy bears."

Bea looked at the ceiling and back at him. "So, I over-reacted?"

"Maybe a tad." Pete put up his fingers, measuring a sliver of space between them. "But..."

"Oh, thank goodness because I thought this was..." She shook her head. "I do love you, you know that. As a friend."

Pete had learned to hate the word friend, especially when it came out of Bea's mouth. But he pushed his feelings aside, swallowed them down like those pills he'd taken earlier, and made the rest of the pancakes. Bea took her pain meds with the water and sat down, pouring syrup all over her pancakes before digging in.

They sat at the small table for two and talked about everything except them. That had become the norm lately.

Pete moved in the following week.

They lived together for seven weeks before Pete decided that he was going to be honest with Bea and tell her that he was going to move out. That he needed some space away from her and his feelings for her. That maybe friendship wasn't an option since the feelings he had for her weren't fading.

She had never promised him anything but friendship. This was on him, not her. Plus, he had an opportunity that might pan out to something more in the snowboarding world, but it meant he had to leave here...leave Bea.

He grabbed them dinner from a sushi restaurant they loved, so it wouldn't be the worst night of his life if Bea got upset with him.

Bea walked through the door, and Pete immediately saw that something was wrong. He hugged her as he usually did when she'd had a shitty day at work. She was struggling to find what she wanted to do for an occupation, and the office jobs she was taking were horrible.

He sat her down at the table, poured her a glass of wine, and brought out the sushi from the fridge.

She stared at it, then looked at Pete. "Is this some test? A joke?"

Pete was baffled. "What?"

"You always know what's going on with me, so did you purposely buy this to pry it out of me?"

Pete was clueless. He grabbed his chair and slid it across to sit right in front of her. "I have no idea what you're talking about."

Tears flooded Bea's eyes and cascaded down her cheeks. She shuddered out a breath, and her crying quickly got out of control. "I'm..." Another deep breath.

Pete wanted her to spit out. He couldn't handle being in the dark, and he felt sick at seeing her so upset and not knowing what he could do to fix it.

"I'm...pregnant." She buried her head in her hands, inconsolable.

Pete leaned back in the chair as thoughts piled up inside his mind like a heap of garbage.

A baby. She was having a baby. His baby.

Everything he had planned that night flew out the door that Bea had walked through moments ago.

I pull into my driveway after sneaking out a back door of the resort instead of going through the lobby. I don't need to be back on Buzz Wheel's radar.

Harper is still at Palmer's when I drive up to my house. I knock, and Harper already has her coat on when she answers the back door.

"Hey, Romeo," she says with a grin. "Give me five." She raises her hand.

"What are you talking about?" I ask, not returning the high five.

"You're not fun." She lowers her hand. "You think you can keep something from me? I know the two of you were getting all hot and heavy while I was watching your kid."

Fuck, no way did Palmer tell her, but then again, Harper, along with Linus, are the cousins Palmer is closest to. It could be a good sign or a bad sign that she sought out advice from Harper. Who knows what she told her?

"Don't get upset. Linus called me last night. You were missing your white horse, but kudos, buddy. I love the fact that you busted in there and broke up their date."

I feel my cheeks redden. I owe Matt an apology for what I did. All this time, I told him I was cool with it, then their first real date, I break it up and end up sleeping with Palmer. "Did you talk to her about it?"

Harper can't lie. She gives away so much with her face, so I really hope no one asks her point-blank if Palmer and I are sleeping together. She glances at her car in Palmer's driveway. "I have to go. Adley's having her nap, and the monitor is on." Then she walks toward her car.

"Harper?"

She rocks her head back and turns around with an exaggerated movement as if I'm nagging her, and she's a sixteen-year-old. "Whhhaaaattt?"

God help me when Adley's a teenager.

"Tell me what she said."

She shakes her head. "My alliance is with Palmer, but I really want the two of you to work out, so let me just say, she's not going to run. That's all I can tell you."

That's enough for me.

I smile. "Thanks. Bye."

I step inside and shut the door, not waiting for her to respond. When I turn and look through the window, Harper narrows her eyes and flips me off before walking to her car.

I laugh and walk into the family room. The monitor is on the coffee table, but I head upstairs and peek into Adley's room. She's fast asleep, giving me some time for my own nap. After last night, I need the rest.

I sprawl out on the couch, but before I try to nod off, I pull out my phone. I need to get this conversation over with.

Matt answers on the first ring. "Hey, prick," he says with a lightness in his tone.

"I just wanted to apologize."

"Don't worry, I poured all my angst into a hot blonde I met at the bar." He laughs.

And that's why I didn't want Palmer to be with him, although I don't think she was looking for anything serious with him.

"Still. I gave you the green light and then shoved you out of the car. Not cool on my part."

He's silent for a moment. "Just do me a favor and don't blow it. You guys obviously have feelings for one another, and I get that emotions run hot. I have no idea why you didn't get together sooner. Don't let the little shit get in the way. I say that as a child of divorced parents who have each remarried twice."

"Thanks, man."

"I'm serious, Hudson. I get you're all hot for one another right now, but the lust will fade, and you don't want Adley to be collateral damage. "

"It's not like that. Not for me."

"That's good to hear. I just remember you back in the day."

I shake my head. "Listen, could you keep it to yourself about Palmer and me? Like you said, we're going to take it slow and not tell Adley or anyone else for that matter."

"Well, you're already in Buzz Wheel."

I laugh. "You're seriously reading that?"

"Yeah. I like it. See you Monday."

"Later."

We hang up, and I drop the phone next to the monitor, grabbing an afghan from the back of the couch and laying it over me. Being this tired after the night I had with Palmer is worth it. It feels as if I've been waiting a lifetime for this.

AN HOUR LATER, Adley's talking through the monitor, so I open my eyes, wishing I had another two hours to catch up on my sleep. I turn off the monitor and climb the stairs, then open her door.

"Daddy!" she says, sitting up in her bed.

Maybe I could've let her stir for longer, but she jumps down and runs over to me. God, to be able to wake up in the same house as her every day would be amazing. I hold her tightly, standing and bringing her up in my arms.

"Where's Mommy?"

"Working." I walk out of her room and down the stairs. "It's just you and me, but Mommy said we're going to have movie night tonight."

"YAY! *Elemental!*"

I groan because we've watched that movie a thousand times, I swear.

"Maybe. We'll see what we have." I lower her to the floor. "Let's get your coat and go to the grocery store so we can make our own pizzas tonight."

"OMG!"

I stare at my little girl, knowing she could've only learned that phrase from one person. Jesus, Harper. "You want something to drink or eat before we go?"

"Juice, please."

"Sure thing." I ruffle her hair that's a little out of control, but we don't have time to do it since it usually takes me forever because of my big clumsy fingers. She'll have to go out looking a tad disheveled.

We head to the grocery store, and I swear everyone in Lake Starlight is shopping today.

A teacher who works with Theresa passes me in the

produce aisle and gives me the evil eye. "You should be ashamed of yourself. You embarrassed her enough."

I blow out a breath. Luckily, Adley is distracted in the cart with my phone.

I say nothing. I probably never should've entertained a relationship with Theresa, but I'd given up on anything happening between Palmer and me.

I should've gone to Sunrise Bay to do my shopping because the minute I go down the sauce aisle, I stop and try to step back, but Theresa catches me in her peripheral vision.

Fuck.

She doesn't say anything, placing the jar she was picking up from the shelf and putting it in her cart. It's like seeing a wild cat at your back door. I'm not sure what to do. How do I react? And seriously, does every teacher shop here after school?

Adley drops my phone, and I scramble to pick it up, hoping Theresa will be gone when I stand, but then Adley says, "Theresa."

Shit. Shit. Shit.

"Hi, Adley, how are you?" Theresa approaches us like a cat ready to pounce on its dinner.

What is she going to say? No way she'd make a scene in front of Adley.

"Look at my nails." Adley raises her hands, showing off the color.

"How pretty. Did Daddy paint them?" Theresa glances at me briefly, then her eyes fixate on Adley's hair. She rolls her eyes and huffs.

"No. Harper did." She smiles innocently at Theresa.

I let the two talk about colors, standing there like an idiot, unsure of what to do or how to act.

"And it's movie night. Me, Mommy, and Daddy."

I love Adley's excitement, but right now, I wish she'd go back to the phone.

"That's nice." The strain in Theresa's voice is obvious to me.

"And make our own pizza. Daddy, I want pepperoni."

"I know. We'll get it." I ruffle her hair.

Theresa doesn't say anything, and I'm unsure what she's expecting.

I clear my throat. "It's um…"

"I'm not stupid, Hudson. I know who you spent the night with." She looks at Adley, who has picked up my phone again and is watching her kid's show.

"Stupid is a bad word," Adley says, not looking away from the phone.

"Adley—"

Theresa interrupts me. "You're right, it is. You shouldn't say it, and I shouldn't either. Well, I should go. Have fun tonight."

"Theresa—"

She puts up her hand and walks away.

So we're not there yet. Good to know.

It's weird to feel so awkward with someone I've slept with. With someone who, before last night, I talked to almost every day. But I don't regret it.

I'm grabbing the cheese when my phone vibrates, and Adley passes it to me. "Text."

It's crazy what these kids pick up about technology so easily these days.

> I'm packing up and see you at home.

> We're leaving the grocery store in ten.

Perfect. See you then.

The three dots appear as if she's going to send another message and I stand in the refrigerated section waiting like a dog for his treat, but they disappear. My heart sinks, but I remind myself, it's early days. I hand the phone back to Adley and head to the cashier.

Of course, Theresa is one lane over, and word must have traveled fast that we broke up. It hasn't been in Buzz Wheel that I know of, but the way the cashiers look at each other tells me that gossip in Lake Starlight is alive and kicking, and everyone knows Theresa and Hudson are no longer.

I can't get out of the parking lot fast enough, so I quickly get Adley strapped into her car seat. On the drive home, Adley tells me about her time with Harper. Although Harper is a little crazy and has some growing up to do, she's great with Adley. Never complains about playing a game, painting nails, or baking. She does it all with Adley.

Palmer's car is in the garage when I pull into my own. After getting Adley out, I grab the bags and Adley walks toward my house.

"No, we're gonna do it at Mommy's," I tell her.

She exaggerates circling back around and heads toward the back door of Palmer's house. I open the door, and Adley stands on a chair to help me unpack the groceries. Palmer walks into the kitchen with her hair piled high in a bun, pajama pants on with a sweatshirt and fuzzy socks.

I love this look on her, I always have. I wish I could wrap my arm around her waist and kiss her fiercely, showing her how much I missed her today.

"Pizza, Mommy!" Adley takes out the pepperoni and holds it up. "Pepperoni. What goes on yours?"

Palmer wraps her arms around Adley from behind and nuzzles her face into her neck.

"Mommy!" Adley squirms, but Palmer only holds her tighter.

"I missed you," she says.

Adley turns around and puts her arms around Palmer's neck. "I missed you, Mommy." Then she slides down from the chair. "I gotta go potty."

It's the perfect excuse for me to have a little privacy with Palmer.

When I hear Adley peeing, I know I only have a couple of minutes. I tug Palmer into my arms and place my lips on hers. Just the kiss causes my dick to perk up. I want her so badly, but the sink in the bathroom turns on, and Palmer tries to slide out of my hold. I grip her harder, pushing her against me so she can feel through those thin pajama pants what she's doing to me.

"You're playing dirty," she whispers against my lips.

"Of course I am." I kiss her again before pushing her away right before Adley walks into the room, holding up her hands.

"All clean."

Palmer's cheeks are red, making her even more of a temptress. "Let's go then."

The three of us make our pizzas, and we make Adley sit at the coffee table to eat her pizza, while we're on the couch. My hand slides under the blanket over Palmer's lap a few times, but she shoos it away every time. Tonight is going to be pure torture.

After we finish eating, Adley comes up on the couch, sliding in between us. Midway through a bowl of popcorn, Adley takes one of Palmer's hands then one of mine, bringing them into her lap so the three of us are holding hands together.

I look at Palmer, and she looks as if she might cry. Adley turns to Palmer and then me, leaning back on the couch with a goofy smile. Palmer stares over Adley's head at me, and I can hear her thoughts as though she's yelling them, the worry that keeps her an arm's length away from me.

She doesn't have to tell me what she's thinking. *We can't break her, Hudson.*

Her fear is real, and it's a valid concern. But what if it could be so much better than what we thought we could have?

<h1 style="text-align:center">twenty-three</h1>

PALMER

The cabin is slowly becoming my second home. I light a candle that I bought at the farmers' market last year and brought with me. It smells like a man's cologne, and I'm hoping it will help me channel Pete for his point of view in my story.

Because though this story needs to be written, I'd really rather spend my day with Hudson. He doesn't have any lessons this morning and wanted to spend Adley's time at preschool in bed with me. It was tempting and hard to deny him, but I have to finish this book.

When I saw the email from my editor this morning, it made my decision for me.

The sooner I knock this out, the sooner I can spend my free time with Hudson, so I tell myself that today is worth spending the time writing.

Bea knew Pete wouldn't abandon her. She couldn't remember if they'd used a condom and it broke or if they hadn't bothered at all with protection in their drunkenness. When she was one week late, she chalked it up to stress. Stress about losing Pete after they had hooked up. Stress that he was now her room-mate. Stress that she didn't have a clue what she was going to do with her life. When her period didn't come by the third week, something inside her told her to take a test and here they were. Her crying while Pete tried to assure her everything would be fine. She had to get a grip.

She wiped her tears from her face with her palm.

"Are you sure you're pregnant?"

She laughed, although it was sarcastic and not fair to him. He hadn't seen the six tests she'd taken.

"Stupid question." Pete shook his head. "Do you know what you want to do?"

Bea hadn't thought of anything except how similar this all seemed to her mother's story when she was pregnant with her. Other than the fact that her mother was madly in love with her dad, and they were together at the time. Until...Bea didn't want to go into the past again. All it ever did was conjure up hurt and anger. As everyone always told her, she had to get over it.

Her hand landed on her stomach. Although there was no movement from the little being growing inside her, she knew there was only one decision to be made. She picked up her head and exhaled a deep breath. "I want to have the baby."

Pete exhaled hard and sat down on one of the chairs, no expression on his face.

"You don't have to...I mean, I'll go home and raise the baby. You don't have to be involved. I don't want to force this on you." She thought she was giving Pete an out, but he sprang from the chair so forcefully it toppled back, banging against the floor.

"What?" Pete walked away from her, tugging at his neck. He didn't say anything else. He didn't look at her. He didn't do anything except stare at the wall.

Bea's stomach clenched. Was he mad at her? Because it took two people to get here. She knew he had dreams of making it in the snowboarding world, that he had been spending a lot of time perfecting his tricks, and a baby would throw a kink in his plan. Neither of them made nearly enough money at their jobs, but surely others with less made it work.

"Talk to me," she said in a near whisper.

He turned around, and she'd rarely seen the expression he wore on his face. He'd certainly never looked at her with it. He was livid, and she didn't understand why. Her defensive side had her straightening her back as she prepared for a fight.

"In all the time you've known me, how could you think I wouldn't be there to help? That I wouldn't stand at your side? That I wouldn't hold your hand when our child is born? Fuck, Bea, this pisses me off." He stormed into the kitchen, and she followed.

He grabbed a beer from the fridge, cracked it open, and downed half the bottle. When he slammed it on the counter, she was surprised it didn't break. As she processed what he was actually angry about, she realized she had underestimated him, and he was right to be upset.

She knew this man. How could she think he'd do anything other than support her decision.

"I'm sorry. I just don't want you to feel trapped." She wrapped her arms around her stomach, nausea rumbling hard.

He shook his head. "It's not ideal. I think you agree with me on that since you cried when you told me. But it's our baby, Bea. Half you and half me." His gaze fell to her stomach. "I'd never walk away from you two, and I thought you knew that about me. I thought you trusted me."

Bea flinched at the word trust. She knew she had no good reason not to trust the people in her life. But she still always expected the worst of them. She was always waiting for the other shoe to drop, for people to prove to her that they weren't who they said they were. She was sure they'd disappoint her if she gave them all of herself. The lie about her parents that she'd discovered at fourteen had shaken her to her core. But Pete had never done one thing wrong.

"I do trust you," she admitted. Walking over, she slid her arms around his stomach. "I trust you, Pete."

He was one of the few people in the world where that held true. She hadn't realized it until just that moment. When she saw those positive signs on all the tests, she'd had a gut feeling that Pete wouldn't walk away from her now. But that seed of doubt always sat in her subconscious mind, waiting for anything to nurture it to life.

She looked up at him. His arms lay limp at his sides. "I'm sorry. Can we start this over?"

Pete's eyes met hers, and a slow smile creased his lips. "Yeah." He sheltered her in his arms. The warmth of that hug felt like home. "We'll figure this out together."

Bea allowed all the alarms in her head to quiet, or maybe it was Pete who silenced them. All she knew was that she'd do anything for this little one growing inside her body and she'd never take him or her away from their father.

I SHUT Adley's door quietly and tiptoe downstairs. I find Hudson on the couch, sprawled on his back, remote in hand.

"When did you get here?" I ask, walking over to the couch with a smile.

He holds out his hand, and when I accept it, he tugs me down on top of him. "I knew you were putting her to bed, so I snuck in." He drops the remote on the coffee table and his warm arms wrap around me. "I missed you."

"I missed you too."

He quirks an eyebrow. "Tell me about the book. How's it going? You seem like you've really hit your stride."

I don't want to talk about the book. Lately, I've realized how similar the story is to Hudson's and my own. It's embarrassing, and I'm not sure how he'll handle it. I know I have to talk to him about it. Especially before it's published, if it's published—my editor may say it sucks.

"How were your lessons?" I change the subject.

From the small shake of his head, he knows what I'm doing. He slides so his back is pressed against the back of the couch, and I lie on my side. His fingers tease the patch of skin above my waist. "Fine. The usual whiny kids and grown adults on holiday."

I laugh, remembering the stories he's told me about adults being worse than the kids. "Do you ever wish—"

He places his fingers over my lips to silence me. I've asked him this same question a million times, and he never wants to answer me.

"Hudson?"

His body sinks into the cushion. "I would never trade this life." Placing a hand on my hip, he sits up on the end of the couch. "I'm not gonna lie and say Matt being here hasn't conjured up some 'what-if' thoughts."

I sit up and bring my knees up to my chest. "Yeah?"

He slides closer, tugging my arms from around my legs. "But this, us, our family, is number one."

"You could do the halfpipe," I say.

The day I found out I was pregnant was the last day he ever did a run on the halfpipe.

"Never. We both know how dangerous it is."

During that year and few months that we hung out before we came to Lake Starlight, I did witness a lot of injuries among the guys he hung around.

"But—"

"Will you please stop?" He cradles my face with his hands. "I'm exactly where I want to be. End of discussion."

He kisses me, and I lose my train of thought. Everything else evaporates. I lower my legs, and he leans his back along the couch, bringing me over his lap so I'm straddling him. Our tongues tangle and a fluttery sensation ghosts across my skin. A low whine squeaks out of me when he ends the kiss.

"This is so much better than trying some hard-ass trick on a halfpipe."

"You always say the best things." I grin at him.

"Only to you." He leans forward and places his lips on mine again.

I wish I didn't always think I took him away from his future. I wouldn't trade Adley for anything, but I'm living my dream as a writer. When I hear him complain, I feel guilty. And if I have him, then I have everything a girl could want.

Hudson strips his lips from mine and gives me a look as if to say, get out of your head, we're making out here.

"I'm sorry."

He sighs. "When will you believe me?"

"I do. I mean, I know how much you love Adley." And I do know it. That's the truth.

He leans back and locks eyes with me. I look to my right, feeling a tad vulnerable. He lightly grasps my chin and brings me to face him again. "And I love you. I'm not sure you understand how happy this has all made me. I've waited a long time to get this chance with you, Palmer. I want a future with you and not as the co-parent of our daughter. Sure, I pushed away my feelings a long time ago, thinking you might never get there."

"She comes first," I say for what feels like the millionth time since we found out about her.

He chuckles, but it's not hearty like when we're messing around. "Always. But you need a life too. You need love too. Let me love you, Palmer. That's all I ask. Just let me in."

My hands slide up his torso and around his neck. "Hudson, I've let you in more than anyone else."

"I know, and thank you for that. But open up the rest of the way for me. Give me all of yourself, and I promise I'll give you a life filled with happiness."

I can't deny how scared I am to let him have all of me, but one thing I learned from my parents after I found out the truth is you can't accomplish anything halfway. If I really want this to work, damn the consequences, I have to put everything into it.

"Okay," I say and kiss him.

He closes the kiss right away, and I groan. "Finally. Fuck, you're a hard one."

I giggle, and his fingers fiddle with the hem of my T-shirt, sliding under and coasting up to my breasts. Our kisses become more urgent. I really wish we could have sex, but Adley is just upstairs. So we settle for a heavy make-out session with a lot of touching.

We lie on the couch until one in the morning, talking and kissing and just enjoying one another. Our long goodbye at my back door is excruciating since I want to take him to my room, but we promise to get a night alone soon.

I flick the lock on the door.

"Mommy."

I circle around so fast I get dizzy. Adley stands there in her pajamas. *Why are you up?*

"I peed," she says and breaks down crying.

I rush over and pick her up, taking one last look at Hudson walking into his house.

Who am I kidding? He had all of me a long time ago. There's no playing this halfway to protect myself from getting hurt. I love that man.

twenty-four

HUDSON

It's been a month since Palmer and I started sneaking around. We barely get any alone time since that would entail asking her parents or Harper to babysit. Sometimes I wish my family didn't live in the lower forty-eight. We sometimes manage to have some time alone during the day if Adley is at preschool, and I don't have a lesson to teach, but Palmer has to finish her book so even that time is cut short.

Just as I'm thinking how I can make it happen, my phone dings.

27 Cottagewood Drive NOW

?? Was this meant for me.

Yes.

She includes a picture of herself. Not showing anything, but it insinuates that she's naked, at least on top.

Don't you dare move.

I grab my keys and run out to my truck, speeding out of the driveway. Unfamiliar with the address, I put it in my GPS when I reach the first stop sign. It says it's along the lake but on the other side. I didn't even know this road existed.

I follow the directions, winding through the hills along a road that's not for the inexperienced. Her SUV is parked on a gravel driveway in front of a little cabin that has a lot of character. Is this where she's been going while writing her book? Her secret place?

I park my truck next to her SUV and climb out. I'm a tad skeptical as I walk along the pathway and knock on the arched door. Peeking into the window, I can't see anything because the drapes are pulled shut.

The door creaks open, and Palmer peeks her head out. "Welcome."

I step inside. "Where are we?" The question dies on my lips when I see that she's wearing a lacy purple baby doll lingerie set. "Fuck, Palm."

"Do you like it?"

"Is that really even a question?" I pull her to me. "You better take these off. Is it okay?" I touch her cochlear implants.

"Of course." She removes her left one while I remove her right.

She leads me by the hand to a small bedroom in the back with only a queen-sized bed and a dresser.

"What is this place?" I ask, forgetting that she can't hear me or see my lips.

She stops at the edge of the bed and turns around. Her fingers fiddle with my belt as I search my mind for any explanation as to whose cabin this is. My pants fall to the floor, then Palmer falls to her knees in front of me, hooking her fingers on either side of my boxer briefs and tugging them down my legs.

Who the hell cares whose place this is? She's at eye level with my dick as I step out of my pants.

Palming my dick, she looks up at me. I try to convey with my eyes how much I love seeing her there.

She slides me between her lips, and shit, the warmth of her mouth makes me buck. Her tongue twirls around my shaft as she grips the base with her hand. She sucks, and my eyes close at the best sensation in this fucking world. Her head bobs and the sound of her saliva coating my cock echoes in the small space.

My hands itch to grab her head and fuck her mouth, but I clench them at my sides, barely hanging on. She keeps up the pace or gets faster, I'm not quite sure, but she works me until my balls draw tight. I want to come in her mouth so badly, to watch her take it all. But she's wearing that lingerie, and I have the desperate urge to be inside her.

She looks up at me with her big eyes, and I stare at her. She's so gorgeous and sexy—I can't believe she's mine.

"It feels so good."

She must read my lips because she pulls herself off my dick and smiles before pumping and bobbing and sucking again. Unable to hold back anymore, I touch her face. She looks up at me again.

"I'm going to come," I say, and she nods, not moving off my dick.

Fuck, she's going to let me finish in her mouth.

A rush of heat travels up my back. I think of nothing but her and what she's doing and the euphoria ripping through my body. I finish in her mouth, and she swallows all of it.

My head rolls back, and my eyes close as I finally unleash the built-up tension.

She licks me clean, and I almost become hard again watching her. I urge her up and she comes willingly. I press my lips to hers, tasting myself on her tongue. Picking her up, I toss her on the bed, and she squeals.

She's the picture of alluring perfection sprawled out on the bed with her long dark hair cascading over the pillow and a flirtatious grin on her face, the lace fabric teasing me with what's hidden underneath. My knee lands on the mattress and it dips from my weight. We have an hour before I have to get Adley, and we're going to make the most of that time.

Just as I lie on top of her, ready to kiss her, there's a knock on the door.

I rear back, and her eyes widen, probably wondering about the shocked expression on my face.

"Someone's at the door," I say so she can read my lips.

Then there's the sound of a key in the lock. I bolt up and slam the bedroom door, grabbing for my pants.

"What the fuck?" I say, but Palmer doesn't hear me because she's pulling a bag from the closet and tossing it on the bed. She shoves on some joggers over the lingerie and throws a hoodie over top.

I trip trying to get both legs into my pants and fall on the floor.

"Yoo-hoo!" a woman says. "Palmer?"

I stare at Palmer as she finger-combs her hair. Shit. Her cochlear implants are in the other room.

She walks across the room, laughing quietly. *Stay here.* Then she slides out the door, shutting it behind her.

A minute passes in which time she must put her

implants in because I hear her say, "Alice, what are you doing here?"

Alice? As in Alice from Northern Lights Retirement Home? What the hell?

I GET DRESSED, sit on the bed, and try to listen to their conversation.

After a few minutes, I question why I'm even hiding. My truck is parked outside, so surely Alice saw it.

While I wait to be let out of the bedroom, I look around the room, and finally, the pieces of whose cabin this might be come together. I see pictures of Palmer's great-grandma Dori. I never got to meet her, but the family tells a lot of stories about her. I think I would have really liked her. Palmer has a picture in her family room of her with her great-grandma, so I recognize her. The man with Dori must be Palmer's great-grandfather. So this was their place? How come I never knew about it? Palmer has never said anything to me.

I pick up my phone to kill some time, but I have no signal. I look up the Wi-Fi, but the network called Big D's is password protected. Great. I huff, resting my back on the headboard.

My eyes catch on Palmer's duffle bag strewn open on the bed, some clothes haphazardly shoved in. Her laptop peeks out. I reach for it. If she's been working here, she must be on the Wi-Fi. I'll surf the net or something to pass the time.

I situate myself on the bed and open the laptop. Her manuscript comes up, but I click on the internet. I've been wanting to get Adley a swing set for her birthday this year, so I search for a local place to check it out. Between all Palmer's cousins and me, we should be able to build it with no problem.

Her manuscript tempts me though. I don't want to pry, but I love reading her work, and she's been so secretive about this book. Usually she's asking for my opinion on different plot points or ideas she might have.

Reading a few paragraphs isn't going to hurt.

Bea's abdomen was getting bigger by the day and her libido was off the charts. She wanted to have sex, and the more she watched Pete around their apartment, the more her body screamed at her for not taking him to bed.

She didn't want to give Pete the wrong idea. She knew he had feelings for her that went deeper than friendship, and no matter what, she wouldn't toy with him. She had to put the baby first.

If she was truthful with herself, she'd admit that she loved Pete as more than a friend. There was no denying her attraction to him that first night at the bar. If Sarah hadn't showed up that night, Bea wondered if they'd be a couple right now.

I frown, sitting back against the headboard. Is her story our story? It's all so similar. That first night, my crazy ex showed up at that diner, knocking out my headlights. She had been clingy from the beginning, and I should've seen the writing on the wall. Palmer retreated after that, and I'd felt the wall go up, blocking me out.

I scroll down a few pages and read more.

Bea was a nervous wreck. She'd lost her job and knew no one would hire a person as pregnant as she was. Who was going to take the time to train a new employee when that employee was about to go on maternity leave? She'd been at home all night while Pete worked at the bar. She wrote down a list of options for herself, but she only saw one real one. One which wasn't ideal.

How was she going to tell Pete she wanted to go home? She —they—needed a network of people to help them if they had any chance of making it. But she'd already taken away his snowboarding dream. She didn't want to force him into a small town he had no link to or desire to be in.

She grabbed some food from their favorite Mexican restaurant and set it up on the small table. As she arranged the table, waiting for him to come home, she convinced herself that he didn't have to come with her. He could be involved in her life with their daughter as much or as little as he wanted, but she had to go somewhere with help.

The door opened, and her stomach clenched. Now was the moment she'd been dreading since coming to the conclusion to return home.

Pete set his keys on the table by the door as always, and she heard him get out of his boots, placing them on their mat. And when the pads of his steps rang out, she thought she might throw up.

He came in and smiled at Bea, his gaze falling to her stomach. She felt his love for their child grow with every inch she grew. He'd place his hand on her stomach sometimes when they were watching television. He talked to her stomach and played music to it. At times, Bea felt jealous of the attention because, until this point, she had been Pete's sole focus.

But she'd ruined her chance with Pete. Her fears had kept her from taking the chance of being with him. Now, this little girl who kicked her endlessly was priority number one. She needed a mom and a dad who loved one another and didn't hurt her with their drama and issues. Bea could not afford to complicate their situation any further than it already was.

"Hey, what's this?" Pete took in the table and looked at her quizzically.

She could admit she didn't do nearly as much as she should for Pete. "I got us dinner."

He didn't say anything right away, but his smile dropped. "What is it, Bea? Is she okay?"

There was honest fear darkening his eyes. She couldn't hold off anymore.

"I want to move back to my hometown." She ripped off the Band-Aid, and his fearful look transformed into misery. Her heart missed a beat as she waited for him to respond.

"When do you want us to move?" he asked.

Yeah, she'd made a big mistake last year when she'd friend-zoned him. Pete was a catch, and she had been stupid enough to let him slip through her fingers. But at least she knew she'd always have him in her life now that they'd share parenting duties. Not ideal, but at least she didn't have to give up the one person who knew her best and accepted all her faults. That was hard to come by.

I scroll a little more, and the character Bea returns home and surprises her family with the news of her being pregnant.

This is our story.

I listen again and still hear Palmer talking to Alice and some other people. God knows who.

She's writing our story, and if it's true, that means Palmer felt the same way Bea did. This entire time, I thought she didn't have any feelings for me. That this revelation we'd come to was all new to her, but has she loved me the same way I have her all this time?

I can't help but grieve the time lost but hope springs out of that grief. We're not going to lose any more time with this wishy-washy crap. What I have in mind is bold, but this time, I'm not going to shy away from what I want with Palmer.

How could I forget that Alice wants me to attend their book club meeting? Of course, rather than picking up the phone like a normal person, she decided to ambush me at the cabin. Calista needs to get the key away from her. Luckily, Alice bought my excuse that my car wouldn't start so I was driving Hudson's truck and still had to get mine towed to the shop.

"I love you, Palmer, but I'm not going to Northern Lights," Hudson says while browning up the meat for tacos that night.

"Come on. I never ask anything of you."

With raised eyebrows, he glances at me at the kitchen table.

"Fine, but what if they talk about the sex scenes? I can't deal with that on my own." I finish my read-through of my latest chapters and send them to my editor then shut my laptop.

I get up from the table and peek in on Adley. She's playing with her toys, pretending she's cooking in the little toy kitchen Hudson got her.

With her being distracted, I walk over and wrap my arms around Hudson, one of my hands venturing south and grabbing his dick through his jeans.

"I'll repay you. On my knees," I whisper in his ear.

"Using all the tactics, huh?" He seasons the ground beef. "I'm going to make sure you make good on that promise."

"Mommy!" Adley comes in, and I rush away from Hudson, but she stands there and stares at us. "Why are you touching Daddy?"

Hudson is no help, turning around and biting his lip. He glances at me from the corner of his eye, probably about to laugh.

I was just hugging Daddy.

Her face twists. "Theresa hugged Daddy."

Oh? I act surprised.

"I didn't like it."

I have no idea how to react. *Sorry?* I sign to buy time.

She comes over and hands me a Barbie. "I can't get it on."

Thank God she's moved on to a new topic, but I hate these Barbie clothes. How do they expect a little girl to dress the doll when a grown adult can barely even do it?

"Barbie wants to go dance, but Ken said no." Her facial expression makes a laugh bubble up out of me.

"Why would he do that?" I ask aloud since my hands are occupied with this stupid doll. I loosen the sleeve of the dress to slide up Barbie's plastic arm.

"Because he likes Skipper's Mommy."

My hands stop, and I give Hudson a help expression. He ignores it and continues to cook the meat.

"Oh, well, maybe they can go together."

Hudson coughs out a laugh.

"Daddy broke Theresa."

Barbie drops from my hands.

"Mommy!" Adley bends down and picks up the doll. "Now Barbie has to go to the doctor." She walks out of the room, and I bury my head in my hands.

Hudson releases his laugh. "Way to break Barbie, Mommy."

"Shut up." I playfully punch his bicep. "You were no help."

"What was I supposed to say?"

I shake my head. "You're coming to Northern Lights with me tomorrow. I'm going to call my mom to babysit." I grab my phone out of my purse and pull up my mom's name.

"Ask her if she can keep her for the night."

"Why? Bedtime at Northern Lights is probably early."

He laughs again. "The Northern Lights residents are unlike other people their age, you know that."

I shrug and nod. He's got a point. They're not your typical elderly people in a care facility. The stories my aunts and uncles have told us all about when Great-Grandma Dori lived there are unbelievable.

HUDSON and I drop off Adley at my parents' house and drive across town to Northern Lights Retirement Center.

"You know they're going to make this uncomfortable for me," I tell him on the way in.

"It's the only reason I agreed to come." He grins.

I stare blankly, and he laughs, putting his arm around my shoulders and kissing my temple. When I circle out of his hold, he grunts.

"This is the hub of the gossip circle," I remind him.

Over the past month, our relationship has only grown stronger, sweeter. Adley seems happier, which makes me wonder if something did shift when Theresa came into our lives, and it happened so slowly I just didn't notice. The time we spent as a family diminished. Now we spend every night together as long as Hudson doesn't have night lessons.

Eventually, Hudson won't be cool with the way things are, and he's going to want to tell Adley. And I can't blame him. I always tend to lie on the side of caution, whereas he's more a "trust his gut and go" type of person.

We walk into Northern Lights, and Leeann, the person who works behind the desk, smiles and waves. "They're all ready for you in the meeting room."

"Should I be worried?" I ask.

She hems and haws. "With that crew? Always. But honestly, not to scare you, they were talking about the sex scenes, so that might be a topic they want to explore."

"Good times," I say.

She laughs. "At least you have your bodyguard with you." She eyes Hudson. "Then again, he might cause more commotion. Everyone is still gossiping about your night alone at Glacier Point." She arches an eyebrow at him.

"Well, people need to learn my business isn't theirs." There's a bite to his tone, but he plays it off with his panty-melting smile that works on Leeann. Even if she's twice his age.

"Have fun." She sits down and continues whatever she was doing before we walked in.

Most of the people in the meeting room are in chairs or have been wheeled in in their wheelchairs, and they all look at us with anticipation when we walk in. Alice beelines across the room to greet me.

"Palmer! Oh." She stops when she notices Hudson. "You brought your muse too?"

I look at Hudson, and he chuckles. "He's not my muse," I say.

Some kind of small noise comes from Hudson. What is that about?

Alice winks dramatically. "Okkaayy."

"No, really." This is not starting off on the best foot.

"Come. Come." She saunters over to the front of the room where one lonely chair sits. "Gilbert, grab that other chair. She brought Hudson, her muse."

I inwardly groan. This is going to be as traumatic as I thought.

"Would it be that bad if I was your muse?" Hudson whispers.

"No, I'm just...I don't want to do this," I whine like a child—like Adley, in fact.

"It will be over fast."

Hudson takes the chair from Gilbert. He used to be our town lawyer, and from what I know, he's most of the residents at Northern Lights's lawyer still. He's dressed in his classic wingtips and a three-piece suit with a pocket watch and chain. A classic elegant and sophisticated look. He takes a seat next to Alice, a guy in sweatpants and slippers next to him.

"Sit!" Alice says a little forcefully, and Hudson and I sit as though we're children at church. "Introduce yourself."

My cheeks heat, and I glance at Hudson, who gives me an encouraging smile.

"Hi, everyone, I'm Palmer Ferguson."

"She's a Bailey. Sedona's daughter." Alice turns in her seat to inform the room.

Okay then. A few of them whisper, which I'm used to. The Baileys always seem to be gossiped about.

"And I'm an author." I clear my throat. "A romance author, and from what I hear, you picked my book this month. Alice asked me to join you tonight, so I'm here."

Not my best introduction, but whatever.

"Yes, I have the list of questions here." Alice pulls a pad of paper from a bag resting at her feet.

Panic races up my spine. How many questions could she have?

"The sex. What's the inspiration for that?"

"Um…"

Hudson laughs, and when I shoot him a look, he turns it into a cough. Jean, Alice's sidekick, rushes over and fills a water glass for him. I mentally roll my eyes.

"It's not really based on inspiration," I say.

"Come on, it has to come from personal experience?" the guy in sweats asks. "And let me tell you something, you're one lucky lady. Not everyone is lucky enough to have sex like that."

My cheeks get hotter.

"You're a pervert, Melvin!" a woman shouts from the back.

He leans forward. "How do I get the ladies to…you know? Your character happily went down on—"

"Oh shit," Hudson whispers.

I give him another scathing look, even if he can't save me.

"Maybe I should clarify that I write *fiction*." I give them a wan smile, hoping that will get us off the topic. "And I like to think my stories are about more than just sex. They're about love and hope and finding the one person you want to spend your life with."

"Honey, we're all late in the game here. We don't have a long life ahead of us, and we'd like to experience as much happiness as we can," Melvin says.

"I don't need someone to harp on what I'm eating and whether I'm walking or did I take my pills," Melvin continues. "I just need someone to give me a little pleasure."

A woman two rows from the front raises her hand. She has on red glasses that match her hair, and she appears very grandmotherly. She'll turn this conversation back where it should be.

I point at her and nod. "Go ahead."

"You said the guy was very big. How big? What is the average size? Because I only slept with my late husband, and I always felt he was on the smaller side. You wrote that he"—she points at Hudson—"barely fit in her. My husband used to slide right out."

My mouth hangs open. I have no response. Like none. Hudson puffs out his chest as if I was writing about him. Not that his size is anything to complain about.

"Once again, he"—I point at Hudson—"is not my muse. He's my best friend."

"And the father of your daughter. So you've slept with him, no?" Jean asks, eyeing Hudson as though he's cheesecake after dinner instead of the usual sugar-free Jell-O.

He squirms, and now it's my turn to laugh.

"Yes, but it doesn't work like that," I say.

"What I want to know is about that position they had sex in. I'm not sure I can get my hips in that position. I had one replaced a decade ago, you know. Will you show us what exactly you were describing?" Alice asks, and Gilbert smiles widely at her.

No. No. No. This is my worst nightmare coming true.

Alice stands and gets into the position I wrote in my book. When the heroine was bent over the couch and had one leg up so he could get deeper into her. "My hips don't go like that, but your description of how deep—"

"Okay." I stop all the conversation and take a breath. "You're only focusing on the sex and not the love story."

"The sex was the only good part," Melvin says. "No offense."

I purse my lips. "Fine. You want to see it? Here is it!" I grab Hudson and drag him over so we're next to Alice. I bend forward over the table and raise my leg so my knee is resting on the table. "Grind me."

"Um...no," Hudson says with a look of horror.

I take his hand and place it on my hip. "Just give them what they want so we can get out of here."

He steps closer to me, and Alice stands to get a closer look, Gilbert joining her.

"If I do this, I cannot guarantee my reaction." Hudson tilts his head, warning me.

"Just do it. I want to get out of here," I whisper.

He comes in behind me and places his hands on my hips, grinding his pelvis into my ass.

"In the book, he grabbed her hair and pulled her head back," a woman in the audience calls.

"Pull my hair."

"Palmer, this is out of control." But Hudson winds my long hair around his fist, careful with my cochlear implants.

"This is it," I say loudly enough for all of them to hear.

"But our hips..." Alice complains again.

I lower my leg. "Just bending and widening the legs will be practically the same."

I go into that position.

"I tap out," Hudson says, stepping back.

"And he's not her muse." Melvin guffaws. "I knew that whole 'my car is broken down' thing was bullshit the other day." He points, and everyone looks to where Hudson is trying to adjust himself.

Hudson gives me a well-deserved death glare, and I nibble the inside of my cheek. Jean looks as though she's going to cry, and I'm about to join her for many different reasons.

I didn't notice Leeann at the back of the room, but she claps to draw everyone's attention. "This has been enlightening. There are refreshments on the table. Alice tells me that Palmer and Hudson have agreed to stick around for any private questions."

Wait, what?

"Are book club meetings usually sex lessons?" Hudson asks. "You owe me huge for tonight."

Hudson is the least of my problems because I'll pay him back with tons of sex, and he'll be fine. My bigger problem is Melvin is walking toward me, pulling out a piece of paper.

"I'm gonna go get a cookie," Hudson says, but I grab his shirt and tug him back.

"You can eat my cookie later. You're staying."

"Want to give them a lesson on eating out?" Hudson asks and laughs.

"I saw this online, should I buy it? Do you have one?" Melvin asks when he reaches us, and he hands Hudson the piece of paper.

He unfolds it, and it's a printout of an ad for a penis enlarger.

"Jesus," Hudson says and eyes me.

Yeah, I owe him big.

twenty-six

HUDSON

A few more weeks pass, and I grow antsy, wanting to out us. We've almost gotten caught by everyone we know, including Palmer's mom. At first it was fun, sneaking kisses and finding secret places to fuck. Hell, Adley woke up one night to find me between her mom's legs. We made up an excuse that I was helping Palmer find something she'd dropped.

We're probably scarring Adley for life.

Most of all, I want to sleep—not have sex, sleep—in a bed with Palmer. I want to see her right before I shut my eyes, hold her tightly all night, and kiss her awake in the morning. I want us to start our life together.

Palmer isn't great at telling people what she wants, so the manuscript I read with a story so similar to ours keeps repeating in my head. Maybe she does want it all, but she's scared to admit it to herself.

Which is why I'm standing in a jewelry store in Anchorage with Harper next to me.

"Have you guys talked about this?" Harper asks, putting

a ring the saleswoman is showing me on her hand and admiring it.

"No, but it's the next step. What do you think of that one?"

She takes it off. "Are you sure she wants this? I mean, Palmer has always had different thoughts about marriage than most women." She picks up a princess-cut diamond ring. At this point, I think she just wants to try on every damn ring in the store.

My gut says this is where we should be going. Harper isn't wrong—neither Palmer nor I have ever felt as though we needed a marriage license with whoever we ended up with. We both feel it doesn't change anything, doesn't bind two people together any more than they already are. But I've never felt like this before. I've never wanted someone to have my last name. To have a corny sign on our door with a last name we all share.

"I guess I'll find out when I ask her. You're still good to watch Adley this weekend?"

She eyes me, and I see the skepticism all over her face. "Of course. I bought a neon pink nail polish she'll love."

"Thanks. And you can keep her at your place?"

"Sure. Do you want any help with the plans?"

"No. I've got it covered." That's an easy one, because Palmer isn't one for flashy public displays.

"Can I see that round one with the small diamonds on the side?" She points at the ring in question in the glass case.

"Are you looking for yourself or Palmer?" I ask what I've been wondering for the last hour.

"Palmer, of course," she says, but I don't believe her, and I don't think the saleswoman does either. "I wonder what it must be like to wear this kind of symbol on your hand so that the whole world knows that someone loves you enough to spend a small fortune on you. Like he wants to show the world that you belong to him."

The words ring true, and I realize that's another reason I'm standing here—I want everyone to know Palmer is mine and how much I love her. Who would've guessed that Harper knew my reason for being here better than I did?

"A hopeless romantic, huh?" the saleswoman asks her.

I've never thought of Harper as a hopeless romantic. I always assumed she didn't want to settle down because of what an active sex life she has. I thought she loves her life, not being attached to any one guy. But what if all this time she's just been searching for the right guy?

"Nice guys are hard to come by," she tells the lady. "Last one. The pear shape please."

The saleswoman pulls out the pear-shaped diamond ring on a platinum band, and Harper and I turn to each other.

"That's the one," we say in unison.

I take it from the velvet mat and examine the unique way the band is thicker, the two diamonds on the side bigger than normal. It fits Palmer perfectly. "Package it up please."

"Did you want to try it on for him?" the saleswoman asks Harper.

"*No!*" we say at the same time.

"That's only meant for one person to wear." Harper looks at me.

I completely agree. It's Palmer's ring, and it will never be on any finger but hers.

The saleswomen goes to polish and clean it and package it up.

"Thanks, Harper."

"Always happy to help, and I won't tell a soul, but you should know rumors are swirling. People already suspect something is up with you two, so coming out as an engaged couple...people might say 'I knew it.'"

How on Earth do people know anything when we're so good about sneaking around? I'm so over Buzz Wheel.

"I don't care what other people say or think."

She nods. "I know. That's why you're perfect for her. Always have been. She should have listened to me sooner." She walks away while I go to pay for the ring.

Signing my credit card receipt, I think about the look on Palmer's face when I propose to her. Harper's questions about whether I'm making the right decision surface, but I push away the doubts.

ADLEY WENT over to Harper's place, and Palmer thinks it is so we can have some time alone. Turns out having houses right next to one another isn't ideal when you want to sneak around, and you have an almost four-year-old. Adley's constantly going from house to house, so there are no sleepovers. But hopefully after tonight, that all changes.

Last night, I made an elegant dinner, and we watched a movie, made love, and talked for hours about nothing and everything. I held her in my arms the entire night, kissing her skin every time I woke.

She's still sleeping, so I sneak downstairs to set my plan in motion.

I make pancakes because I want to give her breakfast in bed. Had I known all those years ago what our life could be, I would've proposed sooner. Forced Palmer to see how good we can be. But I push all that shit and wasted time away and walk up the stairs with a tray full of pancakes, butter, syrup, and juice.

I take a deep breath, opening my bedroom door where Palmer is still sprawled out asleep. Not ready yet, I watch her for a few moments, then I place the tray on my side table and crawl into bed with her. She moans and stretches, her usual catlike one. I can't wait to see that every morning.

I grab her cochlear implants next to the bed and put them on her. "Good morning." I kiss her briefly.

"Good morning," she says, eyeing the tray of food. "You've been busy."

"I have." I grab the tray and place it on her lap. "Enjoy."

"Pancakes." She sighs and smiles at me. "Share some of mine?"

"I will, but you start."

She picks up her knife to butter her pancakes, and my heart pounds. There's no turning back now.

She lifts the first pancake and pauses, staring at the ring. "What the?" She drops the knife and picks up the ring, turning to me. "What is this?"

I take it from her hands and kneel on the mattress, sitting back on my ankles. "Palmer Ferguson, you stole my heart at the bar on the night we met. I tried to give it away to others, but I was foolish to think it could belong to anyone but you. I love you and only you, and I always will. Will you marry me?"

She picks up the tray and puts it by her feet on the bed. "Hudson..."

My heart sinks into my stomach.

"We don't need a marriage license. You didn't need to spend that kind of money on a ring. God, how much did it cost?"

I lean back, speechless.

She must see my expression, the two of us able to read each other's minds all too often. "I mean, we've talked about how being married doesn't stop anyone from cheating or making mistakes. It doesn't make that person any more yours. It's just a piece of paper."

"Things change."

She shakes her head. "They didn't. I don't need the state of Alaska to give me a certificate so I know I love you. I only need you to know it and believe it." She gets up on her knees, facing me. "And I do love you. So much. So much more than I ever thought I could fall in love with someone. I've fought my demons, fought the urge to run away from this."

"Exactly. I want you to be my wife. I want you to have my last name. I want everyone to know how much I love you, how much we love each other."

She scoffs. "A piece of paper doesn't prove that to people. Them witnessing our love, being around us will have them seeing how much we mean to one another. Standing in front of a group of people and promising each other a bunch of things isn't love."

Fuck, Harper was right. My chest squeezes to the point that it's hard to breathe.

She grabs my hand and brings it to her heart. "This is yours. You own my heart, Hudson. But I don't want to wear that much money around my finger just to prove to others that you love me. I don't want some big wedding where we spend all Adley's college fund to show off that I found the perfect man. I like our life as it is now."

I retract my hand from her chest. "You like sneaking around?"

Her head rolls back. "What does sneaking around have to do with getting married?"

"I don't want to do it anymore. I want us out in the open. I'm done with looking around corners and spending every night alone in my bed. I want to tell Adley. You're so concerned about money? Well, we have two mortgages that could be one."

"You're changing the topic," she says. "The two things have nothing in common."

"Actually, they do. It's you keeping me all to yourself and not wanting the world to know about me." Anger boils inside me, and I clench my hands to keep calm.

"You're acting like a baby because I said no to your proposal."

My phone vibrates on the side table, but I ignore it.

"A baby? You refuse to tell people about us. Why is that, Palmer? Because then maybe if you do decide to run, it'll be easier. No witnesses." She blinks a few times, but I keep going. "Or maybe you think that if this doesn't work out, and we don't make it, somehow you won't hurt as much because the people you walk by on Main Street won't know that we were dating in the first place. You know what amazes me? You've lived here most of your life, but you don't realize that people see it. They see us together. The way we look at one another. The way we parent our daughter together. They know. Without us telling them, they know. You're living in a dream world."

She looks as if I slapped her—probably because I've never gone at her like I am right now.

"I know you want all this, but you won't admit it to yourself. When I was at the cabin, I read some of your manuscript."

"You what?"

I can tell she's pissed, and she probably has a right to be, but that's not the point right now. "That's our story you're telling. I know how you feel about me, how you've felt from the beginning."

My phone vibrates again, interrupting me. I reach for it in case it's about Adley, but it's work. It goes to voicemail, and less than a minute later, it chimes, letting me know there's a voicemail. I press the button to listen to it and put it on speaker.

Palmer stares at me, her mouth open. "Seriously? You're checking your voicemail right now?"

"It's work. You know, how I paid for that damn ring that I get to return now."

She throws her hands in the air. "You made a rash decision."

I ignore her, listening to my boss. Raul is out sick, and he needs me to come in. I text him that I'll be in. The last place I want to be is here with Palmer right now anyway.

"I have to go." I scramble to grab my stuff and get dressed.

"Hudson, someone else can do it. We're in the middle of something."

I shake my head. I need to calm down before we have this conversation again. I need to figure out what kind of future I want with Palmer and whether I can accept what she wants. "Later. I have to go."

I change my clothes. She watches me the entire time, but neither of us speaks. After I'm ready to go, I hesitate by the door, unsure what to do. I glance at the ring on the night table, the diamond shining from the stream of sunlight coming in through the window.

"Hudson?"

"Not now. I need time. I'll be home later. You'll get Adley?"

She huffs. "Yeah, but—"

I walk out of the room, downstairs, and outside to my truck. I start it up and pull out of the driveway, stopping when I get to the stop sign and taking in a deep breath as my fist pounds the steering wheel. I'm frustrated with Palmer and even more frustrated with myself.

I press on the gas, hoping the more distance I put between us, the more the pain in my chest will loosen.

twenty-seven

PALMER

I sit on Hudson's bed and blow out a breath.

Why would he think he should propose? Everything with us has been great. I haven't been holding back, I've been giving him everything, but marriage? We always agreed that marriage wasn't necessary for either of us.

The ring shines on the ceiling, and I roll over, grabbing it. It's gorgeous. He couldn't pick one more suited to me. The urge to slide it on my finger is strong, but I deny myself. If you don't want a marriage, you don't get the ring.

I shove it in the drawer of the dresser, get up, make the bed, and grab my bag. His second story is small, just his room, Adley's room, and a bathroom. I peek into her room, which he recently redid for her with a ladybug theme. She has as much stuff in here as she does at my house. Even though we've lived separately all this time, there's still a divide. Days when she's not with me. Which would be fine if I wasn't in love with her father.

I sit on her stool and grab one of her stuffed ladybugs, hugging it to my chest. What is wrong with me? Sure, I don't believe in the whole marriage thing, but the panic that arose when I saw that ring shouldn't have caused the knee-jerk reaction it did.

Hudson loves me and wants to announce it to everyone we know and people we don't. That's not a bad thing. It's something most women dream of.

Shaking my head, I put the ladybug stuffed animal on Adley's bed and walk out of the room and down the stairs. My hand brushes the hanging pictures of Adley and Hudson. I'm in a few, but it's mostly just them. Our daughter looks so happy in each one. We've given her a good life so far, and all I've done is worry that I'm messing up. But she's well-adjusted and happy most of the time. She'll deal with her dad and me coming out as a couple, and she'll deal with it if we don't work out. Have I been using her as an excuse this entire time?

There's so much to process. I figure I'll bury myself in my work and deal with it later. I open the back door to return home and freeze.

Theresa stands there with a box in her hands. Her eyes widen. "I'm sorry. I was just...these are his things. I was just returning them."

I stare at the box. His things, stuff he left at her house while they were together. The thought that he had a drawer at her place brings bile up my throat. I want to grab the box and burn everything in it, destroying the evidence that he was ever with another woman.

"Can you give it to him? I didn't see his truck, so I was just going to leave it at the door. I thought it was safe." She hands me the box and walks back to her SUV.

"Theresa!" I call, dropping the box on the step and walking toward her.

She stops and turns around, seeming surprised that I'm

speaking directly to her, because I never did when she was with Hudson. "You don't have to soften the blow. I think I've always known."

I tilt my head and try to decipher what she's talking about. "I just wanted to apologize."

A condescending laugh erupts out of her, echoing around us. "Apologize? You know what? The two of you need to get your shit together. You're hurting people because you don't want to admit what you feel for each other. I always saw it. I was just stupid enough to think I could change it."

"What?" I ask, baffled because we were just co-parents. It's not as if Hudson was sleeping with me while he was seeing her.

"The way he looked at you. I knew I'd never compare, but..." Her shoulders rise and fall. "I'm competitive by nature, so I probably thought I could win him. That one day he'd look at me like I was his entire life."

I don't know what to say, so I stand there like an idiot. "I—"

"I'm fine. I don't need your pity or his or anyone else's. But I'll give you one piece of advice. I'm not sure why the two of you play this game you do. I can only think it's because of Adley. But kids are resilient, and the happier their parents are, the happier they'll be. Whether her parents are together or not. I admire you guys for trying the co-parenting thing and intermingling your lives, but there's doing it for the child and doing it for yourselves. I think you both should take the time to decipher who liked this arrangement you came up with more, you or Adley?" She opens her SUV door, and I stand there watching her drive away.

I pick up the box, take it inside, and place it on Hudson's

kitchen table. There's a T-shirt, a razor, a bottle of his cologne, and some other random stuff. I stare at it and chew the inside of my cheek. He doesn't need any of this, not anymore.

I pick up the box, walk out to the garbage cans, and toss it in. That was his past, and I'm his future.

I head inside my house to write the ending of my book. The ending that should have happened earlier today, but I was too stupid to realize I wanted the same thing he did.

I WRITE the end of the book, send it off to the editor, and a weight lifts from my shoulders. Sure, she'll come back with edits, and I'll be revisiting that manuscript, but the first draft is complete.

I slide my laptop into my case and spot Great-Grandma Dori's letter where I've been carrying it around since it was given to me. I never did read it. Maybe I should have. Maybe I wouldn't have ruined all this with Hudson. Sitting on the couch, I slowly open the letter, still not ready to read her last advice to me, but it's time, I know it is.

My Dearest Palmer,

You remind me so much of myself. Your resilience, your fight, your stubbornness. All great traits, and if anyone tells you differently, tell them to go to hell.

I understand how upset you got with your parents when you were younger. How badly it hurt that they'd lied to you and made you believe love was easy because of the example you saw growing up. But kids aren't supposed to see the struggles of their parents. They made amends when you were eighteen months old and put that part of their lives in the past where it belonged.

So what if your mom left your dad because he couldn't stop drinking? It sobered him up. Your dad should have sought out help before letting it get that far, but he lost a career that was his passion and was what would feed you and your mother. He came to Lake Starlight and won your mother back because he wasn't afraid to admit to his mistakes, and he put in the hard work to fix them. That's all that matters.

One day, you're going to find a man and the two of you will have your struggles. Everyone does. But you'll get through them—together. Your parents' struggle was just one small part of their love story, not the whole thing.

You deserve the world, Palmer, but if you're not careful, fear and stubbornness can cause you to live a lonely life.

You've been a fighter your entire life. You've

had to be. I'm so proud of the woman you became. Always fight for what you want.

I love you, and I'll miss you.

Please come home. You've been gone way too long, and your mom misses you.

Love always,
Great-Grandma Dori

I fold the letter back up, her words echoing Theresa's. I need to fight for Hudson. For our future. For our daughter. Great-Grandma Dori's right—I never used to be afraid to take what I want.

My back door opens, and I walk over to greet Adley with tears in my eyes, but it's not Harper or Adley. It's my parents. What the hell?

"Palmer," my mom says with that tone implies she's not happy with me. I realize that she's cut her hair shorter, and it suits her.

My dad holds a tray with three coffees and a bag from Brewed Awakenings.

What are you guys doing here? I have my cochlear implants in but it's habit to sign when its just my parents and me, a lifetime of conditioning I suppose.

Neither of them answer me, taking a seat at my table. My dad hands out the coffees as my mom pats the spot across from her. *Sit down, Palmer.*

Did someone die?

Jesus, no. Sit down. My mom pats the spot again and sits back in her chair.

I hesitantly go over and sit across from them.

I received some information this morning.

"Oh?" I look at my dad, but he's not giving away anything.

There's something you don't know, Mom signs. *No one knows except your father. And the secret needs to stay with you.*

I'm baffled. This is not usually how my parents are. They're usually straightforward. *Another secret.* I roll my eyes.

"Palmer, let it go." My dad uses his stern voice, as if I'm sixteen and giving my mom attitude.

"I write Buzz Wheel," she says out loud.

My mouth falls open, and I gasp. *I'm sorry, what? You're the one who spreads the gossip about all of us?*

She nods. *And I'm not going to apologize for it. I haven't always written it. It was passed on to me when I was younger. But that's not the point. The point is that someone wrote in that you and Hudson have been having a secret relationship.*

I shift in my seat.

Listen, we know you harbor some anger over what you found out at fourteen, but we want to know why the two of you would sneak around and not just be open about it. You have a daughter together, my dad signs.

You don't have to worry about it, we're going to come out. As long as he accepts my apology.

Mom looks at Dad and they share an expression like, "Of course she fucked it up."

What happened? my mom signs.

I look at the table. "He might have proposed."

"Which explains the other piece of information I received."

I look up at her.

We'd hoped he hadn't asked you yet so that we could get to you first. She looks at my dad again.

What did you hear?

Mom sips her coffee then sets it down. *Hudson was spotted with Harper at a jewelry store in Anchorage a few days ago. The person thought Hudson was with Harper, but I knew that wasn't true.*

Harper, of all people, knows how I feel about marriage. Why didn't she clue him in? Or me for that matter?

Which is what has spurred our surprise visit. We wanted to see where your head was, Dad signs.

I messed up big time when he asked me. I'm sorry that I'm such a basket case.

You know that's not it, Palmer. We take responsibility for you and your trust issues. We're trying to guide you in the right direction, my mom signs.

Hudson is a good man. He loves you—

I put up my hand to cut off my dad. *I don't need a lecture or a talking-to. I told him no, but I'm going to rectify that as soon as he gets home. I have a plan, and it entails us coming out.*

"But, honey—" My dad thinks I'm still that pissed-off fourteen-year-old who googled his name and found out the truth. And maybe I was her for way too long. But not anymore.

No, Dad. I'm over it. You're right. Hudson is a great man, and I love him. And wearing his ring and holding his name isn't so we can prove it to other people. It's about belonging to someone. I see now that's why he asked me. I was just a little late on the uptick as usual.

My parents laugh, and my mom's head falls back, a deep relieved breath flowing out of her.

That's good to hear. But are you sure he'll take you back? My mom looks concerned.

My dad chuckles harder, grabbing her hand. "He'll take her back. That's love, forgiving one another. Right, lass?"

My mom gets all googly-eyed at my dad and nods. "That's right."

Now we can have the danishes. My dad opens the bag they brought.

"I'll grab a plate." Mom gets up from the table and heads to the cupboard.

Movement outside draws my attention, and I see Harper's car pull up in the driveway.

"Perfect timing, here's Adley." I go to the back door and step out, but only Harper gets out of the vehicle. Her gaze goes to my left hand, and her shoulders sink. I have so much to tell her when Adley goes down for her nap. "Where is she?"

"I dropped her at my parents'. I tried to go to yours, but they're here, I see."

Something about her tone and the way she's dodging eye contact sets me on edge. "Harper, what's going on?"

"Let's go inside." She walks by me and opens the back door.

"Harp?"

She disappears inside. I follow her, wondering why my daughter isn't here and what the hell is going on. By the time I reach the dining room, Harper is whispering to my dad in the dining room. His face falls, and he grabs his keys off the table.

"Sedona!" he calls.

Mom comes running into the room.

"What's going on?" I ask, looking between them all.

Harper looks at my dad, and he looks at my mom.

"What is it, Jamison?" my mom asks, grabbing my hand. She must have the same gut feeling I do that something horrible has happened.

"There's been an accident. Hudson fell into a tree well."

"What?" I rush to grab my keys and purse.

"Just wait, Palmer," my dad says. "Someone saw him disappear, and rescue is on their way to him now. You sit tight and wait to hear. I'll go see what's happening."

My dad's crazy. "No, I'm going."

"I'm right behind you," Harper says.

"Girls, I really want you to stay here," Dad tells us.

I look at Harper, and she reads my mind. "Sorry, Dad, I love him and I'm going."

"And I'm driving her," Harper says.

Harper and I rush from my house. My parents come out right after, climbing into the back seat.

"We're all going then," Dad says.

"Put your seat belts on." Harper slams her foot on the gas, reversing out of the driveway.

"Harper!" my mom screams.

"Sorry, Aunt Sedona." But Harper continues to drive erratically and fast, which at this moment, I actually love her for.

All I want is to spend my life with Hudson, so I grip the holy shit handle and hold on.

We arrive at the ski resort and there's an ambulance out front, putting a guy on a stretcher inside.

I open the door of Harper's car before she can fully stop, running toward the ambulance.

"Hudson! Wait!" I scream. Damn, I really need to start exercising more.

Both men stop and stare at me in confusion. It's not Hudson on the stretcher. It's some guy with a broken arm and a bandage around his head.

"Never mind. I thought you were someone else," I say.

"The guy from the tree well?" the patient asks.

"Yeah." I look at him expectantly.

"These guys were talking about that when they arrived. I ran into some lady on the hill. Guess first-time skiers really should stick to the basic runs." He shifts and moves his arm a bit and cringes.

"Where is he?"

A helicopter circles the area above, and I glance at Harper's car. She and my parents are staring at the helicopter. No. That's not for Hudson. It can't be.

I run down the path, unsure where to go.

"Come on." My dad catches up to me and takes my hand.

He drags me in the direction of the landing helicopter, where there's a crowd of people.

"Excuse me," I say, pushing through the throngs of onlookers, needing to reach Hudson who must be waiting for the life flight. I can't process the nightmares running through my head. "Dad?"

"It's fine, honey. I'm sure it's nothing serious."

I burst through the last layer of people, and a crowd of medical professionals surround the stretcher on the ground. My heart sinks into the depths of my stomach.

"Ma'am, you have to back up," the security guard says. "Let them do their work."

"But it's my...boyfriend."

"Boyfriend?" The security guard looks at me as though I have three heads.

"Yes, he was caught in a tree well. Please. I need to go with him." All I can see is them moving the stretcher toward the helicopter, and I panic, pushing against the security guard's chest as he blocks me. "Let me go. I have to see him."

"Please, sir, they have a daughter. Let her see him," my dad says.

The security guard shakes his head. "I'm not sure—"

"Palmer?"

I stop pushing the security guard and whip around. I must be hearing things because...it can't be true. Hudson stands behind me, looking confused.

I run to him, bulldozing into him. He catches me, and I cling to him like a koala bear.

"What's going on?" he asks. "What are you doing here?"

Tears run down my face and all the anxiety inside releases from having him in my arms again.

"Jamison, what's going on?" Hudson asks.

"We thought that was you on the stretcher," my dad answers since I can't.

The helicopter takes off, the wind from the blades whipping up the snow on the ground. I cling to Hudson harder, tighter, afraid to let go.

"That's some woman who hit her head when some guy ran into her. They're taking her straight to the hospital as a precaution because she passed out for a few seconds. I'm fine," Hudson says.

"But you did fall into a tree well?" my dad asks.

"Yeah." Hudson leans back to see me, but I bury my head in his neck. "I got myself out, and they checked me out. I'm good. My arms hurt from climbing, and I have some scrapes, lost my board, but I'm good. Look at me."

I inch back and cradle his face.

He smiles. "I'm here."

"I'm sorry. I'm so stupid."

"And that's my cue. We'll take Adley for the night. You two figure this out." My dad walks away.

I squirm out of Hudson's arms. If they're sore, he doesn't need to be holding me. "Can we go somewhere and talk?"

"We don't have to talk. I shouldn't have asked you to marry me. I just want you in whatever way I can have you. You're right. A piece of paper doesn't change anything."

I shake my head, ready to pour out my heart to him. "Hudson—"

"I just want to go home. I'm exhausted and sore. Drive me home?"

Giving him a small smile, I say, "I'll gladly play nursemaid."

We both head to the parking lot, and he passes me his keys.

"Will you wear that baby doll nightie while taking care of me?" he asks.

I laugh, although this conversation isn't over. I'm going to tell him everything, but I'll let him get his rest first. "Whatever you want."

"I want." He waggles his eyebrows.

He climbs into his truck, and I drive us home, a plan forming in my head. It's about time I show him exactly how much he means to me.

HUDSON SLEEPS FOR THREE HOURS, which is perfect because it gives me time to get everything ready.

When he stirs awake and rolls over, he finds me staring at him. The anticipation of what I'm about to do is so great that I want to do it as soon as he wakes up.

He jolts back. "Jesus, Palmer. You scared me."

"Sorry."

He slowly sits up, his bare chest on display, and I bite my lip because he looks sexy as hell right now. "What's going on? Why are you staring at me like a stalker?"

I grab my laptop from the nightstand and hand it to him. "Read."

He rubs his eyes and blinks a few times. "Right now?"

I slide it forward even more. "Yes, now."

"Okay." He looks at me as though maybe I'm losing it.

"Could you read it out loud? They tell you to read your manuscript out loud to identify any problems."

"Really?" I smile sweetly, and he nods. "Fine."

Pete came into the bedroom carrying pancakes with a hidden treasure under the first one. He couldn't wait to ask her, his excitement already rising to a level he never imagined.

As he always did, he kissed her to wake her, and Bea's eyes fluttered open. She smiled and wanted to grab his face and pull it down to hers, but he asked her to scoot up on the bed.

She caught sight of the plate of pancakes, and her stomach grumbled. Pete was way too good to her, better than she felt she deserved. It scared her, although she tried to push those doubts into the far corners of her brain. They still crept in at times like these. Times when she could never imagine being happier than she was in that moment.

Pete's smile kept growing, and he had this goofy expression she couldn't decipher. He passed the tray to her. She started buttering the pancakes, lifted the top one, and paused. Her eyes examined the ring placed there, and the panic she thought she'd feel in this moment didn't come. All the anxiety over a future with Pete disappeared. Something quieted inside her as she picked up the sparkling diamond ring that was perfect for her.

Pete got up on his knees, and his fingers brushed hers as he took the ring from her. Pete told her how much he loved her and explained how he wanted a future with her. Then he said the words she'd thought would terrify her.

"Will you marry me?"

With a grin, Bea held out her left hand for him to slide the ring on. "Yes, I'll marry you."

Pete slid the ring on her finger and took the tray of pancakes off Bea's lap, bringing her lips to his.

Hudson stops reading and stares at me. "What is this, Palmer?"

I take out the ring and hold it out to him. "Ask me again."

He shakes his head. "I told you I don't need you to marry me. I don't need the marriage license. I can be happy just being with you."

"And what if I'm not?"

His eyes study me for a long time, and I hold my breath, hoping I didn't mess it all up. Sitting up on his knees, he takes the ring from my fingers.

"Palmer, I love you. You and Adley are my world. I want to make a million more Adleys with you. I want the crazy life of a chaotic house so that after we've put them to bed, I can snuggle with you in the quiet of our home and relax. I want to laugh with you when they do and say the craziest things. But mostly, I just want you. I want to love you through all the good and bad this life will bring us. Will you be my wife?"

I wipe the tears falling down my cheeks. "Yes."

He slides the ring on my finger, and I tackle him down to the mattress.

"About time," I joke.

He takes my cheeks in his hands, and I see the question in his eyes. Am I sure? I hope that over time, that question gets answered through my actions.

"God, I love you," he whispers.

"Will you make me pancakes tomorrow morning?"

He laughs. "Every morning for the rest of my life."

I lower my body onto his, and we seal it with a kiss.

PALMER

Six Months Later

"I love my bed," I say to Hudson, hands on my hips.

"And I love my bed."

We're deciding what to merge and what to purge. We agreed to live in my house. Adley made the decision, which was good because I didn't want to move. My place is a little bigger than Hudson's, so it made sense.

The day after Hudson proposed for the second time, we picked up Adley and told her that Mommy and Daddy were going to be a couple and were going to get married. She didn't understand it all, but she loved being the flower girl at our wedding last month.

"Flip for it?" I say, grabbing the quarter we've already used to decide which kitchen table and which couch to keep.

"Whatever, you can have your bed." He waves me off.

I drop the sandwiches for lunch on the table and wiggle between him and the table, straddling him. His hands mold to my hips, and I want to grind, but our daughter is in the other room. "You secretly love my bed."

"Babe, I love any bed you're in."

"You and your sweet answers." I playfully roll my eyes.

"You can have your bed, but I want to bring my chair."

"Ugh, I hate that chair." Not really, but I have to make it appear I'm sacrificing something.

Adley runs in and stops, then groans.

"Come here." Hudson holds out his arm, and Adley runs to his side, where both of us hug her. "My girls."

There's nothing better than hearing those words.

"Let's eat." I move off Hudson's lap, and Adley climbs right up into her chair.

"I have a boyfriend," Adley says after we've started eating.

Hudson chokes on his sandwich.

Who? I try to hold back my smile.

"Holden." She gives us a proud smile.

Well, that's a very grown-up thing. I'm not sure you're old enough.

"No boyfriends until you're twenty," Hudson chimes in.

"He asked me, and I said yes. You said yes to Daddy." She bites her sandwich, looking at us as if confused why we don't get it. "Can he come over for a playdate?"

"No," Hudson answers, shaking his head.

Sure, I'll talk to his mom.

The doorbell rings, and I catch sight of a delivery guy walking away from the door. I get up and open the door and find a small box on the porch. It's a special copy of the book I was writing at the cabin—the one where I altered the ending a bit since it was too close to publication to do with my publisher's copy. Hudson and I will only ever see this copy I had specially printed for us. I pick up the box and bring it over to the table.

"What's that, Mommy?" Adley asks.

My new book. I tear open the box and take out a copy to show her.

"It's your mommy and daddy's love story," Hudson says, taking the book from my hands and thumbing through it.

Adley's nose scrunches up. "Why would someone read that?"

Because we're two people who went through a lot before we figured out what everyone else already knew. I smile at her.

"I knew." Hudson winks at Adley, and she giggles. "Mommy was the one in the dark."

She giggles louder, and I roll with it because I love us, our family.

The back door opens, and Harper comes rushing through, short of breath, continuing on to the powder room.

"What are you doing?" Adley laughs.

I look at Hudson, and we share an expression of what the hell is going on.

The toilet flushes and the faucet runs before Harper comes out.

"Nice of you to stop by," I say.

"It was an emergency. I gotta talk to you."

"Okay, want to have a sandwich first?" I ask.

Her hands fidget in front of her. "Yeah, I should probably eat."

"What's wrong with you?" Hudson asks her, but Harper sits down, ignores him, and starts in on her sandwich.

Adley slides down from the table.

"Where are you going?" I ask her.

"Bathroom."

"Oh wait." Harper shifts to slide out of the chair.

Adley sees it as a challenge and runs into the bathroom, slamming the door.

Harper's hands land on the closed door. "Adley." She fiddles with the handle, but it's locked.

"Relax, she'll be out in a second. Is your stomach upset? Do you have the flu? Because I just sanitized everything after we all had that nasty cold."

Harper isn't listening to me. She keeps trying the doorknob, saying Adley's name over and over. The door opens, and I'm happy the commotion is over.

"What's this?" Adley comes out with a pregnancy test in her hand.

Harper snatches it away.

Hudson spits his water all over the table with a look of fear. Not a great sign for what I was planning on telling him tonight.

I stand from the table, my mouth hanging open, thinking back to when Harper was here a couple of days ago.

Harper looks at the test, then at Hudson. "You!" She points right at him.

My stomach coils, and Hudson's face goes pale, his eyes turning to me. "Is that yours?"

I shake my head. I'm not exactly lying but toeing a line.

"Your friend did this to me," Harper says.

Then I put it all together. The wedding, our wedding.

You slept with the best man? I'd seen them eye-fucking each other a few times, but she never told me she slept with him. I wonder why.

She grunts. "It's false, it has to be. I'm going to buy

more." She walks out of the house before we can say anything.

Adley stands there frozen. "Can I have one of these?"

"No!" Hudson shouts and puts his head down, massaging his temples.

Later that night, after Adley goes to bed, I sit next to Hudson on the couch and hand him my new book, opened to the epilogue.

"What's this?" he asks.

"Read the epilogue. Out loud."

He narrows his eyes but takes the book from me.

Bea and Pete got married in a small ceremony for only their family members. Which didn't end up being that small because there were a lot of family members.

Their honeymoon was amazing, but they came back with a souvenir. Bea worried about telling Pete. They were just starting their life together, and this would bring a new challenge for both of them.

She bit the bullet and sat him down one night after their daughter was asleep, took his hand, and placed it over her stomach, unable to speak the words. She saw Pete's mind working, trying to figure out what was going on until it clicked, and he linked his fingers with hers.

"Really?" he asked.

She nibbled the inside of her cheek and nodded.

A warm, happy smile creased his lips, and he took her in his arms, kissing her. When they closed the kiss, he rested his forehead on hers. "Another baby?"

She nodded again. "Yeah."

He hugged her so tightly she wondered why she had been so worried about telling him in the first place.

Hudson closes the book and raises his eyes to mine, silently asking.

I nod.

He throws the book in the air and grabs me, hoisting me up off the couch and spinning me around. "We're having a baby!"

As I laugh, I'm not sure why I was worried. Hudson is always ready for things before me. If he had waited in the first place, we might not have gotten here, and that would have been the most tragic love story ever.

**Be sure to check out the first book in our new small town series, Plain Daisy Ranch,
The One I Left Behind.**

Retired football star, Ben Noughton returns to his small ranching town, and the woman he left behind fourteen years ago, who wants nothing to do with him.

For those of you who are avid readers of ours and read the ramblings, you know that we tend to write ourselves into corners a lot.

Palmer's book was no different. We wrote Palmer at the end of Lance's book without realizing how similar it was to her mom, Sedona's story, but in the end, we liked the irony in it. Especially if you read Operation Bailey Birthday when Palmer was fourteen. She found herself in a similar position as her mom, with a little different circumstances.

The biggest thing that changed in this book was the hero's name! When he appeared in the bonus scene for The Trouble with Runaway Brides, he was originally named Peyton. But with Peyton and Palmer that got confusing real fast, for both us and all our editors! LOL So we changed it to Hudson and we're happy we did because it really fits him better than Peyton ever did anyway.

Some of you might remember Matt as Grady Kale's rival in Cold as Ice. Originally, we thought he was going to play a more intricate role with Palmer and that she was going to actively pursue him and ask Hudson to help her.

We worried about bringing Matt and Theresa in because we didn't want any love triangles, but we found ourselves in another friend-to-lovers romance and if you know us, this trope puts us on the struggle bus every time. As always, we found ourselves questioning again, why hadn't they crossed that line already? Sure, Adley was a big reason, no parent wants to take a chance that hurts their child. And we had Palmer's wound, but Hudson needed to act, so we needed Matt to show interest in Palmer and create that jealousy. Vice versa with Theresa and Palmer.

We love being in Lake Starlight again and bringing in all the mature Bailey kids. It's always so much fun writing in this world, kind of like going home. Even though we'll always miss Grandma Dori and Grandma Ethel, Alice and her gang at Northern Lights bring their own brand of fun!

A special thanks to our sensitivity readers. Writing a deaf character comes with its challenges and these ladies made sure Palmer's character and the world she as she experiences was portrayed as accurately as possible. Misha Patel, Genevieve Lawrence, Renee Blanchet, and Christie Schauer, thank you for all your feedback!

As always, we have a lot of people to thank for getting this book into your hands...

Nina and the entire Valentine PR team.

Cassie from Joy Editing for line edits and working with us on our timeline when the unexpected happened.

Ellie from My Brother's Editor for line edits and proofing.

Hang Le for the cover and branding for the entire series.

Lindee Robinson for his awesome job of photographing our Palmer and Hudson.

All the bloggers who graciously carve out time to read, review and/or promote us.

Piper Rayne Unicorns who give us a fun space online to chat and show us love on the daily!

Readers – There's so many options to choose from these days and we are beyond grateful that you invested your time and energy into this little world we created.

I'm sure you know who is next. Harper's a little quirky, a little wild, and a little free. We can't wait to dive into her story. And who doesn't love another Bailey baby coming into the mix?!?

xo,
Piper & Rayne

about piper & rayne

Piper Rayne is a USA Today Bestselling Author duo who write "heartwarming humor with a side of sizzle" about families, whether that be blood or found. They both have e-readers full of one-clickable books, they're married to husbands who drive them to drink, and they're both chauffeurs to their kids. Most of all, they love hot heroes and quirky heroines who make them laugh, and they hope you do, too!

also by piper rayne

Lake Starlight

The Problem with Second Chances

The Issue with Bad Boy Roommates

The Trouble with Runaway Brides

The Drawback of Single Dads

The Baileys

Lessons from a One-Night Stand (FREE)

Advice from a Jilted Bride

Birth of a Baby Daddy

Operation Bailey Wedding (Novella)

Falling for My Brother's Best Friend

Demise of a Self-Centered Playboy

Confessions of a Naughty Nanny

Operation Bailey Babies (Novella)

Secrets of the World's Worst Matchmaker

Winning my Best Friend's Girl

Rules for Dating your Ex

Operation Bailey Birthday (Novella)

The Greene Family

My Twist of Fortune (Free Prequel)

My Beautiful Neighbor (FREE)

My Almost Ex

My Vegas Groom

A Greene Family Summer Bash (Novella)

My Sister's Flirty Friend

My Unexpected Surprise

My Famous Frenemy

A Greene Family Vacation (Novella)

My Scorned Best Friend

My Fake Fiancé

My Brother's Forbidden Friend

A Greene Family Christmas (Novella)

Modern Love

Charmed by the Bartender

Hooked by the Boxer

Mad about the Banker

Single Dads Club

Real Deal

Dirty Talker

Sexy Beast

Hollywood Hearts

Mister Mom

Animal Attraction

Domestic Bliss

Bedroom Games

Cold as Ice

On Thin Ice

Break the Ice

Chicago Law

Smitten with the Best Man

Tempted by my Ex-Husband

Seduced by my Ex's Divorce Attorney

Blue Collar Brothers

Flirting with Fire

Crushing on the Cop

Engaged to the EMT

White Collar Brothers

Sexy Filthy Boss

Dirty Flirty Enemy

Wild Steamy Hook-up

The Rooftop Crew

My Bestie's Ex

A Royal Mistake

The Rival Roomies

Our Star-Crossed Kiss

The Do-Over

A Co-Workers Crush

Hockey Hotties

Countdown to a Kiss (Free Prequel)

My Lucky #13 (FREE)

The Trouble with #9

Faking it with #41

Tropical Hat Trick (Novella)

Sneaking around with #34

Second Shot with #76

Offside with #55

Kingsmen Football Stars

False Start (Free Prequel)

You Had Your Chance, Lee Burrows

You Can't Kiss the Nanny, Brady Banks

Over My Brother's Dead Body, Chase Andrews

Chicago Grizzlies

On the Defense (Free Prequel)

Something like Hate

Something like Lust

Something like Love

Plain Daisy Ranch

One Last Summer

The One I Left Behind

The One I Stood Beside

The One I Didn't See Coming

Holiday Romances

Single and Ready to Jingle

Claus and Effect